MW00957961

# DESTINED

USA TODAY BESTSELLING AUTHOR
## SUSANA MOHEL

Destined by Susana Mohel

Copyright © 2022 Susana Mohel

Cover picture: Wander Aguiar

Model: Rodiney Santiago

Editing by: Darlene & Athena @ Sisters Get Lit(erary) Author Services

Proofread by: Ari Basulto & Lucia ToMe

This is a work of fiction. Names, characters, businesses, places, events, locales, and incidents are either the products of the author's imagination or used in a fictitious manner. Any resemblance to actual persons, living or dead, or actual events is purely coincidental.

All rights reserved. This book or any portion thereof may not be reproduced or used in any manner whatsoever without the express written permission of the Author, except for the use of brief quotations in a book review.

The heart has its reasons of which reason knows nothing.

—*Blaise Pascal*

# PLAYLIST

Wrecked – Imagine Dragons

Ed Sheeran – One

Happier – Olivia Rodrigo

Jason Derulo x Nuka – Love Not War

When I Was Your Man – Bruno Mars

Adele – Easy On Me

Heartbeats – Jose Gonzalez

Incomplete – Backstreet Boys

Greatest Love Story – Lanco

MAX & Ali Gatie – Butterflies

# CHAPTER ONE

## *Destinee*

I want a second chance.

Fuck, I deserve a second chance.

I really hope the universe is devising something better right now. People always say the best is yet to come, right?

Trusting in putting my hope in that, I packed my bags, threw them into the back of my car, and drove west, searching for my own sunset. Yeah, that's what I literally did.

"Girl, I hope when you moved here, you brought all your fuck-me heels," Monica, my new coworker says excitedly. "Tonight, we're gonna find you a man, someone who's going to rock your world and give you the warmest welcome. If you get my drift."

Well, if the opportunity for love isn't knocking, then damn, getting laid sounds like the next best thing.

Yes, I like sex. I really enjoy sex. Sex was always the perfect escape, especially when the memories took over and became more than unbearable. Getting laid tonight would be the highlight of my year… or better yet, the best way to end it and ring in a new one. The holidays are almost here, the best time to celebrate with family and friends.

I know it's odd that I decided to move away from my family at this time of year. But after the last couple of months I've had, I realized that I really needed time for myself and time to heal away from any constant reminders—including family. It's been a week since I ventured off on this new endeavor when I pulled up to the front of my new place, ready to start a new life here in Palo Alto. I'm a California girl through and through, right down to my core, staying in the state was always my goal, I couldn't bear to move out of state. I was lucky enough to find this new women's clinic that was looking for a nurse practitioner to join their team of medical professionals. After I applied, they offered me the position and this is my first job after getting my degree. I'm finally putting my education to work. Pretty exciting, right? Every time I think about it, I need to pinch myself.

This isn't my first rodeo in a hospital, in a sense since I previously worked in the biggest one back in my hometown.

"Destinee…" Monica calls out my name, urging me to respond. "Hey, I'm talking to you!"

"Huh?" I ask, breaking me away from my thoughts.

I'm rewarded with the mother of all eye rolls. Monica is one of the nurse's aides who's been working with me all week. She's been a godsend, showing me the ropes, introducing me to the rest of the staff and overall easing me into my new life. So, when she invited me to go with them to a local bar they frequent, I couldn't find an acceptable reason to say no.

"The shoes? A sexy outfit to go for drinks after work?" Monica chastises me. "Seriously, girl, where's your head at?"

I choose to say the truth, at least part of it. "Thinking." The glint of my dragonfly bracelet reminds me that I'm here on a mission. Transform and shine, despite however much it hurts.

"I get it," she replies. "Moving away from your hometown must be tough."

"It is," I say. "But this isn't the first time I've been away from home. I went to college in Davis. It was still somewhat close to home, but living here... this feels different somehow."

"Are you going back to visit for Thanksgiving?"

"I think so," I give her my answer even if I'm not sure yet. Having to say goodbye again... enduring my mother's tears... and attempting to forget that trip to the hospital I'd rather not remember...

"You're such a lucky bitch," she adds. "My family is in South Dakota. I'm not flying home until two days before Christmas, the tickets are outrageously pricey this time of year..."

"Yeah, I'm just a two-hour drive away."

"Anyway," she says while going back to her task with the bags of cotton balls in front of her. It's time to open the doors and start working. We're fully booked for the whole day. For a Friday, our schedule is anything but relaxed. "Tonight, we're going for dinner first, then drinks."

"First things first, we gotta survive this day." At those words, our first walk-in comes through the door.

It's a woman with severe menstrual discomfort, Monica helps me usher her to a room, where we start with the initial examination.

"The pain is getting worse," the poor woman cries, twisting in agony.

I continue with my exam while questioning her. She tells me about the string of specialists she has visited in the last couple of years. "They said it's endometriosis. I've tried every birth control pill known to man. I'd go through periods of time where I just sort of gave up trying to fix it. Getting used to the idea that this is my new normal."

I dislike the idea of a person having to live with this pain, especially if it's treatable. In college, I was very interested in mixing a bit of holistic lifestyle with traditional medicine, so I went for a certification. I know… it's unconventional, and the notion is absurd to some people, too new-age for them. When the boss asked me during the interview, my knees shook a bit, but he was impressed. And hired me, which gives me a bit of free reign to help my patients using other alternatives, besides standard medicine. Connecting body, mind, and soul.

Diet. Exercise. Meditation.

I believe in curing the disease, not the symptoms.

"I'll be giving you a shot for the pain. It will help you for now," I tell her. "But I'd like you to make an appointment with one of our gynecologists here."

The woman, Olga, looks baffled by my suggestion. "The specialists I'd seen before didn't help. Now the pain and symptoms are affecting every aspect of my life. I'm tired all the time; my boss is about to fire me because I've taken so many sick days lately… And I'm not cutting my ovaries out. There is history of heart disease in my family, I don't want to take any unnecessary risks."

My fingers stop for a moment while filling the syringe. I'm sure this woman has endured enough pelvic sonograms in this life and the next. Also, I'm pretty sure she's scared and exhausted. So, I decided to take a different approach. "What do you want, Olga?"

Her green eyes fill with tears. "You know you're the first person who has asked me that?"

It doesn't surprise me. Sometimes medical staff can be a bit pushy. Of course, they are trained, and I'm not judging that, but every now and then it's good to stop and see the patient as a person, not just their ailment.

After that, it's easy to convince her to return. Together we plan a visit with one of the doctors here, I'm sure Dr. Stevens is the right choice for her. After a call to her sister to come pick her up, I give myself a pat on the back. This was the right decision for me—coming here.

And it's just beginning.

By eight-thirty, I've downed at least two—or three—drinks called Pink Panther. I'm relaxed and having the time of my life, laughing at everything my coworkers say. I changed out of my work attire in favor of my favorite jeans and a black top my best friend gave to me as a farewell gift. My hair is down, well, not like I have a lot of options these days. I cut my hair into a very stylish bob before leaving Sunnyville. If I'm expecting to make a change, I bring it into every aspect of my life. I don't do anything half-ass.

We're in a corner at a sports bar. It seems like this one is the place to be because it's packed, and everyone seems happy.

"Don't turn around," Monica whispers-shouts in my ear, a smirk pulling up at her lips. "But seems like your luck is about to change."

"What are you talking about?" I reply with a laugh.

"There is a hunk who has been staring at you the whole time we've been here."

What? I haven't noticed anyone. I pride myself on my observation skills.

What do you do when someone tells you to not look in a certain direction? Of course, I turn to look in said direction. However, Monica is faster than me. And she takes my face between her hands restraining my moves.

"I said *don't turn*, Destinee," she scolded me as if I was a child. "If you want the man to come and get you, you need to play the part and act aloof. Men love a good chase, let him make the first move."

Even in my buzzed state, I know she's right. I'm used to having control, even when I was dating my ex, I always planned everything. Well, everything but the way we ended. It shook me to the core. But it didn't break me.

Mike, one of the family doctors, calls for our attention announcing this round is on him. "Shots for everyone!" he cries.

"And a sparkling water for me," I counter. I need to sober up so that I can manage to get home safely.

"Boooooooo," the three of them jeer at me. "Such a lightweight."

"Hey… you gotta take it easy on me," I reply. "It's my first night out with you guys. I need to work myself up to your level. Don't expect me to come charging out of the gates."

They all laugh at my rant. But ten minutes after leaving the table, Mike comes back, and a bottle of sparkling water appears in front of me.

"Just because you're the newcomer," he announces. "You're welcome!"

After having so many drinks, I excuse myself to go to the ladies' room. When nature calls, a girl needs to answer. I take care of business and wash my hands. While looking at my reflection in the small bathroom mirror, I almost don't recognize the woman staring back at me. She looks so carefree. Without any baggage. Without a broken heart.

Taking a couple of paper towels, I dry my hands and after a deep breath, I head back to the table where my friends are waiting for me.

"He's still there, ya know," Monica says to me while I'm sipping more water.

"Who?"

"The hottie who hasn't taken his eyes off you the whole night," she clarifies. "I told you those fuck-me heels do the trick every time." The pride in her voice makes me chuckle. Being around her is so much fun.

"Ok, mom, can I take a peek now?"

An evil smile spreads across her face.

"Be my guest. He's at eight o'clock," she says, and the moment I turn my head to look at the man, my breath stops.

The noise fades away, and everyone in the room becomes blurry; time stands still. My throat drops to my stomach. No, I refuse to believe it.

It can't be. Not him. Not here.

The past that I'm running from just found me.

# CHAPTER TWO

*Martin*

I'm not drunk. Or high.

It's just my brain playing tricks on me. My fucking brain has been messing with my emotions ever since a blue-eyed girl showed up at my parents' home all grown up and beautiful.

I know that she's constantly on my mind. So it must just be my imagination conjuring her up in a crowded bar far away from the town I know she resides in and loves too much to leave. Destinee Carr, the girl of my dreams can't be here, within reach of my hand.

Then I hear the unmistakable sound of her laugh again. Deep and husky. Even in the busy room, I feel it deep in my bones, sending shivers down my spine. The last time I saw her, golden curls cascaded down her slender back, now her blonde hair is cropped just above her shoulders, and the color is much lighter than before. But those striking eyes surrounded by thick lashes, I'd recognize her mesmerizing eyes anywhere.

"Are you calling dibs?" Finnegan Barnes, one of my VPs whisper-shouts in my ear. "That chick is hot... and most definitely fuckable."

Even though he's speaking the truth, his words infuriate me to the point that I want to behave like a caveman and claim her as mine. Dee looks amazing wearing all black, a sexy top paired with pants that are so tight they look painted on her legs like a second-skin.

I hear myself saying the words before my brain even processes the meaning. "Don't you fucking dare." *She's mine. Even if she has no idea how much I care for her.*

"So, are you making a move or staying here with your ass parked on the stool like a coward?"

Finn has a point. I've been keeping my distance for years now. But what could I do when she was in love with my younger brother?

"I already know her," I tell him without sparing him another look. Fuck it, I'm doing this. I down the rest of my beer and walk to her table where she's surrounded by some people I don't know.

For a moment, our gazes fix on each other and a shiver runs through me once again. Her silvery blue eyes initially spark with heat and then with a hint of shock. She's as surprised to see me as I am to see her.

"Oh my gosh," Destinee cries while jumping into my arms. She feels so right, like she belongs in my embrace. Holding her close gives me the chance to breathe in her intoxicating scent. "What are you doing here, Martin?"

Reluctantly, I pull away to look at her. and I see her bright smile, but it's different to how she's looked at me in the past. She looks less guarded as if she were smiling just for me.

For me—a guy she didn't ever spare a second glance for.

"I should ask you the same," I tell her. "What are you doing so far away from home?"

With sadness shadowing her eyes, she replies, "I needed a change of scenery, Martin. The opportunity came a few weeks ago, so now I'm living here."

That shocks me, I never thought she would leave our hometown. She loves the place, I thought she'd live there forever. Especially since I know her best friend is about to have a baby in a month or so. "Living here? Away from Sunnyville?"

She smiles at me. "Don't be so dramatic, Martin Posada. We aren't that far away, just a couple hours west."

"You're really living here?"

"Well, technically in Mountain View," she laughs a bit, making me smile. "This city is so expensive I couldn't afford to pay three thousand dollars a month for a studio."

She's. Living. Here.' That's the only thing my muddled brain can process.

"My sister never said a word to me." Elena, my little sister, is Destinee's best friend. They have been glued at the hip since they were little girls.

"Your sister's head is in the clouds—a very pink cloud—right now. She barely remembers her own name these days."

That makes me laugh. She's right, my sister is preoccupied with the changes in her life and finding her own happiness.

"So what brings you to the bar?"

"I'm celebrating my first week with my coworkers. Here, let me introduce you." She takes my hand, intertwining our fingers, and turns to face the table, where her friends were looking at us with rapt attention. Now they're so obviously trying to start a fake conversation amongst themselves to feign their innocence.

"Do you want to call your friend over to join us? You left him alone to come and talk to me," Dee says pointing at Finn with a manicured finger.

I don't really want to, but… "Sure," I reply, waving at Finn who is more than elated to join us. Of course, I can tell the fucker has his eyes fixed on one of Destinee's coworkers. A red-haired girl with a southern accent who was introduced to me as Amber.

I start a tab and the drinks start flowing even though I trade in the beer I've been drinking for sparkling water. I'm driving, after all. After a while, Finn and the girl start kissing, the other two girls announce they're leaving to go dancing at a club up the street.

"Wanna go with them?" I ask her, I know how much Dee loves to dance, but internally I'm begging for her to say no. I'm hoping that I'll have the chance to show her my moves later.

"No," she answers almost shyly.

And a bit flirty.

"I'm starving. Want to grab a bite to eat with me?" I suggest, wishing to go to a quieter place with her so we can talk and be alone. This is my chance to make my move. More than that, I'm so ready to get the hell out of the friend zone.

"I can eat."

"I know the best taco place in town." I know she'll agree considering I know what she likes. Destinee has spent enough time at my family home with my sister... then with my idiotic brother David, but I don't want to go there.

"Now you're talking my love language," Destinee says in that sultry voice.

While I settle the check, she goes to the ladies' room, and we meet at the door a couple of minutes later.

"Ready to go?" My hands are tucked in the front pocket of my jeans. Yup, this is the only way of restraining myself from touching her.

For a moment, I go back to being the shy nerdy guy hiding behind thick glasses who is always busy solving math equations, reading *The Lord of The Rings*, or running to go fishing with my fishing rod in hand to the creek behind our home.

Destinee takes hold of my arm as if to absorb my body heat to warm hers against the chill of the night.

"Let me," I tell her while slinging my sweater around her slender shoulders.

Her eyes darken while taking in the sight of me wearing a simple white shirt and dark jeans. I may still be a little nerdy, but it doesn't bother me because I've made something of myself—as well as a ton of money. But also, I've worked hard to get the body I'm rockin'. Right here, in this moment, the hours I spent at the gym are well worth it. The touch of her fingers on my skin are delicate and feel as soft as a feather. This electricity crackling between us, is sending a charge through my body—especially below the belt.

Can a man die from a dire case of blue balls?

"Mmm," she whispers while discreetly clutching my sweater to her nose. "I like the scent of your cologne."

She's flirting with me… She's gotta be flirting with me? But before I make my next move, I need to be sure. I know what happened between David and her. My brother wanted everything the easy way. He only wanted her because she was there, available to him, and always ready to jump at any chance to be with him.

Destinee deserves better than being treated that way.

Since she took an Uber to the bar, I guide her toward my car. She doesn't let my arm go; and I don't want her to because it feels so good to finally have her there. Walking with her, knowing she could be mine. Knowing I'm more than willing to give her the best, starting with the very best of me... Feeling all of this is invigorating.

I know I'm breaking the bro code. Even before I knew I'd have the chance to make her mine, I spoke about this with my older brother, Gabriel, on so many occasions. He's the only one who knows how much Dee means to me— how much she's always meant to me.

And now, months after my last conversation with Gabriel... Here we are—Destinee and I—together.

"I always thought that if you ever moved, it would be closer to David. I know you two..."

She stops in her tracks and looks into my eyes. "David and I are history, Martin," she states with a serious tone. "That's the reason I moved here. I was ready for a change, to start with a blank slate."

Well, that's my opening. The one I was waiting for. Maybe she isn't exactly ready to jump into a relationship right now, but after waiting for her for years, my patience has been tried, tested and true.

I can surely wait a bit more.

That doesn't mean I'd rest on my laurels and do nothing.

Life has taught me that good things won't come if you're a lazy asshole.

I'm a hard-working guy, and now, I'm ready for the fight of a lifetime.

I'm ready to win her love.

❊❊❊

"This is so good," Destinee praises while sipping her drink, *agua de Jamaica.* Or better known as hibiscus-infused water, while a dish with four *carne asada* tacos rests in front of her.

This girl has an appetite, and she's not afraid to own it. I find it so freaking sexy. Everything about her is sexy to me.

"I told you I knew the right place," I reply, giving her a wink.

Destinee blushes, but her gaze is still fixed on me. Dee doesn't have a shy bone in her body, and that's just one of the things I've always liked about her. While growing up, she always forced my homebody of a sister to have fun. Another thing that makes her so lovable is how she comforts those she cares about, for example how she was there for Elena when our mother passed away a couple of years ago. God, she was there for all of us, delivering food and taking care of the house while we were heartbroken, immersed in the fog of the unexpected loss.

"You know at first, your sister couldn't believe I had accepted a position here," she says, talking about her new job in a clinic close to Stanford University. "If I'm being honest, I was shocked too. My mother sulked for an entire week. But that didn't stop me, so here I am."

Her voice sounds chipper.

"I'm proud of you, Miss Nurse Practitioner," I give her praise. "You earned that fancy title."

"Thank you," she replies. "Heck, I'm proud of myself."

"As you should be."

"I'm tired of talking about me," she says. I don't mind since I enjoy hearing her voice, so I've been listening attentively all night. "Now tell me about you, Martin."

Dang, my name sounds so good coming from her sweet mouth.

"There's not much to say. I work a lot, try to visit my father as often as my schedule allows."

That's pretty much a brief summary of my life. Yeah, every now and then I go out with friends, like tonight.

Sometimes I find a woman to fuck… and forget by the next morning.

I'm a single man, after all.

"Really… weren't you just on an exotic island not so long ago?" She asks about my trip to Bali six weeks ago. I went there for a much needed reprieve from my hectic life. "I do follow you on Instagram." She sasses.

That earns her another huge smile from me. This girl.

"And you don't follow me back," she chastises me.

"I plan to fix that immediately," I reply while grabbing my phone from my pocket.

"It seems like you travel often. Tell me about it."

Thirty seconds later, I find her page and follow her back. An image of her smiling, greets me on her profile. She's so fucking beautiful it hurts, and I can't help but to be aroused. Yes, I've been fighting a boner since we were at the bar.

"There's nothing to tell. I really don't travel that often," I answer with a shrug. Having money makes it easy. And no, I'm not complaining. "Would you like to travel anywhere in particular?"

Destinee sighs before answering. "I'd love to, but I've been busy with getting my degree. Now I'm swamped in credit card debt and struggling to pay my rent. There's no way that I'll be traveling anytime soon."

"That's not what I asked." My voice is rougher than I expected. I want an answer because, at the first opportunity, I want to take her to the place she dreams of going.

I want to give her the world.

"Every girl dreams of going to Paris," she whispers. "Me included. Also, I'd like to travel to Italy. Portofino and the Amalfi Coast, visit those villas almost hanging off the rocky cliffs... It looks so beautiful there. You know? Places like the beach, with people drinking fancy drinks while wearing hats and beach attire."

Oh yeah, my imagination conjures up the image instantly. Destinee sipping from a crystal glass in a string bikini, her sun-kissed skin exposed just for me. For my fingers... For my lips...

My already hardened dick is ready to bust out of my pants at just the thought.

"I'd never been there before," I confess.

"Ooh, I want to go to India, too, and attend one of their dragonfly festivals they celebrate at the end of spring. Gah, I love those types of celebrations."

"Are you fond of dragonflies?"

"Yes," she said. This is news to me, I didn't know that about her. "They are symbols of transformation in legends. Two species of dragonflies are associated with the ghosts of two legendary warriors."

Interesting.

"And do you consider yourself as one of them? A warrior, I mean?"

"Yes!" Her eyes are sparkling, and it's hypnotizing. I find myself lost in her glow like the dragonfly she considers herself to be.

I want to tell her how proud I am of her. I want to tell her how beautiful she is to me. I want to tell her how much I want to be by her side. I just want to be in her presence and behold her transformation as she reaches her dreams and shines.

"We should just do it," she says. Her voice is full of mischief. "Let's forget about the rest of the world and fly there tomorrow."

I look at her with a mix of intrigue and surprise.

"You wanna go on an adventure of your life with me?"

"You have no idea," she replies. But in reality she's the one without any idea of where my mind is, since I'm already planning it.

I'll deliver what she's asking for. And more.

# CHAPTER THREE

*Destinee*

I've been drinking and talking all night long with one of the Posada brothers. No, not the one I was in love with ever since I was a teenager, but one of the others.

The guy who always rescued me and took me fishing while I chatted about nonsense.

The guy who now looks like he was manifested from my hottest fantasies.

When Monica, one of my new coworkers, invited me to go for drinks with them, this isn't where I thought my night would end up. The sports bar she chose was packed, and she implied that if I were in the mood to get laid, it would be the place to be, guaranteeing that I wouldn't go home alone. And she was right in one sense… but we'll see where the night takes us from here.

After he came over to our table, everything changed.

I was genuinely happy to see Martin. But he's a reminder of my past, a part that I'd like to forget. I know he's now a bigwig in the tech industry, so what in the living hell was he doing in a place like this? He should be in some fancy as shit lounge sipping imported whisky. Not where we met, in a sports bar with a beer in hand.

Not even in my wildest fantasies, did I imagine running into Martin here.

Gah, why is he so impossible to resist?

"What happened to your glasses?" Martin is very open, answering every question I've asked, even though he seems more interested in knowing everything about me.

"Contacts," he replies.

"No fancy Lasik for you, mister? Too chicken to have someone touching your eyes?"

He laughs, deep and husky. Goose bumps erupt across my arms at the sound.

"More like I've never felt like putting myself through surgery. My glasses don't bother me."

"Does this mean I'll get to see you wearing them?" Why am I picturing him wearing his glasses and only his glasses? Why does my voice sound so flirty? Have I lost my fucking mind?

"You have a nerd fetish?" He questions with a knowing smirk.

Oh my… now he's flirting back. The man looks so edible. His sweater is still over my shoulders engulfing me in the delicious aroma of his cologne while my eyes roam over his arms. And pecs. And all the ways his white t-shirt stretches around his delectable muscles.

And let's not forget about the way he's looking at me. As if I were the appetizer, entrée, and dessert all rolled into one.

"No," My voice, not sounding as confident as the reply implies, and I'm sure he doesn't believe it.

I'm a goner for a guy with geeky vibes. Black rimmed glasses à la Clark Kent with a Superman physique... boom... say goodbye to my panties.

And the guy sitting in front of me checks off all those boxes. He's gorgeous, caring, and charming. And that fucking smile—slays me every time.

If it weren't for the little fact that he's my ex's older brother, I'd be climbing him like a tree. They always say forbidden fruit is sweet and tempting. I feel a bit like Eve, enticed by Lucifer. Tempted and incapable of saying no. Trust me, the temptation is real.

I've been in love with David for as far back as I can remember, but a girl has her limits. And I've reached mine when it comes to him. When we hit our final low, my decision was made. I can do so much better.

I deserve better.

I deserve to be loved by a man who gives me everything. Not a lazy fucker who expects me to do all the work. And to be the only one to make all the sacrifices.

I'm worth more than that.

David couldn't even keep it in his pants. Of course, he laid the blame on me, stating I was never there when he needed me. He said that men have needs, that the girl just fell into his lap. Just like any guy, who's he to deny a warm and willing body, he's only made of flesh and blood.

He called constantly and sent flowers when I ended things, but never took the actual time to see me to face the music. It wasn't enough in my opinion.

"Where did you go?" he asks me, noticing I'm lost in my thoughts.

I shake my head. "Sorry, I was… thinking."

"About?"

"Changes… new challenges…"

"At work?" He's digging for answers.

"No, I'm settling in okay. It's more about…"

"What?"

"Life… my goals… love." Finding my reason to live. To believe again. My parents named me after destiny, like it was fate. Isn't it ironic that I feel like my fate is turning out to be that I'll end up as an old cat lady, alone with only her cats to love and keep her company. But that's not what I want… I want to feel the thrill.

To feel fulfilled.

"Have you figured it out yet?"

"Does anyone ever really figure it out?"

He laughs again, but this time he doesn't spare me a look. He's focusing on the tacos, as if he suddenly finds the *pico de gallo* way too interesting.

"What would you do if suddenly your biggest dream becomes reality?" His intense brown gaze is fixed on me, searching for answers in my eyes.

His question comes as a surprise, since I've never really thought about it. The question paired with his serious expression is leaving a palpable feeling between the two of us, as if he's waiting with bated breath.

I shrug before giving him an answer, trying to sound cheerful and nonchalant. "I don't know... make sure it lasts?"

I'm rewarded with another dashing, big smile. Gosh, what's happening to me tonight? Why am I feeling this way? Damn, those drinks at the bar must be really hitting me.

Suddenly I feel the buzz, a thrill invading me as if something new and meaningful were about to begin.

But why now?

And why with *him*?

Lucifer himself should be getting ready to welcome my soul into hell.

Looking for a distraction, I take the first bite of my taco while it's still hot. Flour tortillas start to get gummy when they're cold.

"Good?" he asks me after chewing his own taco.

"As good as you promised."

"I'm happy to deliver," he replies. His eyes shining with mischief, as if he were laughing at his own private joke.

My gaze wanders around the parking lot. The place I assumed he'd be taking me to is actually a food truck with some picnic tables around it. But I can't complain, the food is amazing.

"These are real tacos."

"Look at you," he says, faking surprise. "Talking about tacos like a true Mexican girl."

That makes me travel back in time. To all those days I spent at his family home, running around the orchard, laughing, and eating. For Mexicans, food means love. They meet at the table and share the meal, chat, and laugh. I've shared many meals with the Posadas. Martin's mother took me under her wing and made me feel like one more in her flock. First as her only daughter's best friend, and then as her younger son's girlfriend. She watched me cry so many times… comforted me while hot tears ran down my cheeks.

And then, when she passed away, Elena continued in her mother's footsteps. She kept feeding me. Including her dried mangoes with chili.

"I learned from the best. Your sister is very picky about her food."

Martin rolls his eyes, "I wish she were just as picky when it came to choosing a husband."

"Hush," I chastise him. "Cardan is one of the good ones and he adores your sister. He's so excited about the baby. They are really cute together."

He ponders this for a moment and hums.

"Cardan was the catalyst for her to get treatment, you know? I can't even think what would have happened without him in her life."

I'm rewarded with another eye roll.

"What? Then tell me what kind of man you would have chosen for your sister?"

He turns to see the people coming and going from the truck. "I don't know, someone like us. A Mexican macho who can hold his tequila and eats real tacos. Not those things in hard shells topped with cheddar cheese…"

I give him a severe look. "So, are you telling me people who aren't Latino can't hold a drink or know about the good stuff? You're sorely mistaken, Martin Posada."

He lifts his hands defensively. "Shit, I'm sorry, Dee. I'm joking. I know Cardan is a good guy. I know the motherfucker loves my sister and makes her happy. As Lena's brother, that's all I want for her," he states, pausing before starting again. "Racial stuff is bullshit, people are people. All that matters is what's inside."

I throw a balled-up paper napkin at him. "You got me there for a second, I can't believe you were just feeding me lies."

He's cracking up. Hard. "I wasn't feeding you lies, just giving you a hard time. You make it too easy."

Giving him the stink eye, I say, "I don't like you that much right now."

"Now, who's the liar?"

Ignoring him, I take another bite of my taco. And another.

"Ready to go?" he asks me after a while. The food on my plate was fully devoured. Not a single crumb was left.

With a hand on the small of my back, Martin guides me to his car. It's a trendy silver electric thing that probably costs as much as a house—something that's definitely out of my price range.

"Are you working tomorrow?" he asks while starting the engine and clicking his seat belt.

"No," I reply quickly. "The clinic is only open from Monday to Friday, so my schedule is pretty relaxed."

"Look at you." He smiles. "Talking like a boss already."

"I said my schedule is relaxed." The clarification should be made. "My work isn't. I started on Tuesday morning, and I've had to deal with a lot already. A middle-aged woman in her first pregnancy dealing with hyperemesis gravidarum and her husband hanging on by a thread. A rich teenager demanding contraceptives... the list is endless."

He clasps my hand in his bigger and warmer one. His touch feels electric. "You're a badass, you got this, Dee."

Just what I needed to hear. "Thank you."

"Hey," he says in a low voice, his body turned to face me. "Come home with me. I'm not ready for this night to end yet."

The air leaves my lungs. For almost a minute, I gawked at him open-mouthed without knowing what to say.

"I'm not asking you over to sleep with me, Dee," he adds, pleading his case. "I have a comfy sofa I can sleep on. Just come with me. We could watch movies or talk all night long... whatever you want. I promise I'll even feed you in the morning."

A smile pulls my lips up. "Are you going to cook for me?"

"I have a couple of talents under my belt that you don't know of... yet," he says with a smirk. His humor helps me to make my decision. I'm going with him, and we'll see where it goes from there.

My conscience can wait until tomorrow to come after me and chastise me to no end.

"Come on. It's not like we haven't slept under the same roof so many times before."

Well, that's true. "But we were at your family home with me sharing your sister's room."

"My bed is bigger and cozier. Imported cotton sheets… and my shower fits…"

Martin smiles, knowing he's winning this little battle between us.

"Shut the fuck up, Martin," I scold him hitting his arm with my open hand. Oh gosh, those muscles are as hard as they look. "You can stop now. I'm convinced, if you keep going I might decide to ditch my tiny place and move in with you."

"So you're coming?" Oh yes, but not in the way I'd like, sadly.

"Ok, Martin," I whisper. "Take me home."

Those words on my tongue taste like the promise of more.

Of what? Only God knows.

# CHAPTER FOUR

*Martin*

While driving toward my house, I keep both hands clutching firmly on the wheel. Trying to restrain myself from twining my fingers with hers while bringing her small, slender hand to my lips—or placing her hand on my lap. Better yet, placing my hand on hers... and moving them farther between her legs...

I know inviting her to my home was a huge mistake. I'm well aware of it. But what could I do? Our conversation had my head reeling and my body humming with need. Lust fogging my rational thinking.

*"What would you do if suddenly your biggest dream becomes reality?" I ask.*

*Her eyes open with a mix of shock and longing.*

*Then she replies with a shrug, "I don't know... make sure it lasts?"*

And I was doomed. I want this night to last forever, even if I'm not fighting the devil who's overtaking my better judgment.

My car moves silently through the deserted street, at this time of night the traffic is light. Soon enough I'm parking my Tesla in the first-floor covered garage. I get out first to rush around the car to open the passenger door for her like the gentleman my father taught me to be.

"You know, you drive a guilt-free car?"

"What?" I have no idea what she's talking about.

"You know, an electric," she says. Her eyes, shining with mischief. "If you fuck someone there…"

Such a bad joke. She has always been the worst comedian, but I find myself laughing anyway. "Yeah, because if I'd fuck someone in my Tesla the first thing on my mind would be the carbon footprint."

Destinee winks with such sassiness that leaves me at a loss for words.

Being with her in the confined space of the elevator is a struggle. My body is screaming for me to corner her and kiss the hell out of those pouty lips. The short ride ends, and I guide her to the door at the end of the hall.

I live on the top floor in a four-story building. When my realtor came to me with the listing, I was a bit reluctant. I was looking for something a bit different, but as soon as I walked through the front door, I knew this was the place for me. Since then, this has been the go-to spot to meet up with my brothers, who often visit. Mostly Gabriel, who lives the closest. Ruben is around a lot, too, considering he's my company's lawyer and often uses that as an excuse to come by so he can challenge me to a game of pool.

If you ask me if I have brought women here before, the answer will be a yes. I'm a guy like any other, far from being a saint.

"Whoa!" she cries out while taking a look at my place. Three thousand feet of living space and an additional private terrace outfitted with high-end everything. Since I planned to live here for the foreseeable future, I spent a good chunk of money making this place amazing. From the beautiful lighting to the furniture, and even to the double-sided fireplace that faces both the living room and the terrace.

Everything is top-notch, no expense was spared. And Destinee notices it.

"This has been a terrible mistake on your part, Posada," she says in awe. For a moment, panic tightens my chest. "I never want to leave. I'll call the movers in the morning."

My smile is so big, it threatens to split my face in two.

"Let me show you my room," I say, extending my arm, signaling the corridor for her to follow me.

"You mean *my* new room, right?" I know she's joking, but a pleasurable feeling fills my chest anyway. She's here, in my home, sharing this space with me. Even if it's temporary, at this point, I'd take whatever she's willing to give. It's a start, but I'll find a way to make it permanent.

Hard work doesn't scare me. And Destinee is a woman who deserves to be wooed, over and over again.

My room is simple in a comfortable and cozy way. There's a big, upholstered bed against the largest wall. The interior designer I hired covered my bed in an over-the-top, showy display of throw pillows that always end up all over the floor just so there's room for me to sleep. But my favorite part is beyond the French doors, a private terrace with a jacuzzi. Since the room faces west, it provides me with a spectacular view of the sun setting over the trees. I'd like to share it with her tomorrow. Shit, that's a lie. I want to share it with her every single night. The both of us naked in the warm water while sipping wine and chatting… fucking… making love.

Making memories.

My cock is straining against my pants. Looking for a distraction, I point to the dresser in front of my bed. "Here, let me grab a t-shirt for you and some sweats."

There is a certain level of trust between us. We have known each other our whole lives. Well, technically since she was five and met my sister in pre-k. Dee used to run around with us all the time, playing in my family's mango orchard. I even helped her this one time to clean her knees when she fell. I attempted to teach her how to fish—it was a waste of time. Destinee was too chatty and impatient to appreciate the art of the pastime, but she took the time to humor me anyway. I was older and didn't notice how beautiful she was until one summer when I came back home from college and found her sitting in the breakfast nook wearing pajamas while talking with my sister and mom.

She took my breath away, and my heart has been hers ever since.

Sadly, that same day I learned she was my younger brother's new girlfriend. David was a year and a half older than her and attended the same high school.

I buried my feelings not wanting to overstep. It was hard not to think about the beautiful girl in front of me—but I did it.

I have kept my distance since then. For years, that was my main focus every time we'd see each other. Until tonight when destiny brought us together. I mean, what are the chances? Finn and I have never been to that place before, and she's here celebrating her first week at work. It's gotta be destiny, right?

"I'm good with the shirt," she replies after a while.

She'll be sleeping in my bed, only wearing one of my shirts. The fuck if that doesn't feed the caveman in me.

In my bed.

Wearing my shirt.

She will be mine.

Is this taboo? Who cares if she's my brother's ex? In all honesty, I don't care what people say. All I care about is her—her happiness.

"Toothbrushes are in the bottom drawer under the counter. Clean towels in the closet… if you need something else just—"

Her hand on my arm stops my words. "I'm not ready to sleep yet," she whispers. "You promised me a movie."

She ditches the sexy high-heels she has been wearing at the foot of my bed and my eyes follow every movement. Her pedicured toes move over the plush carpet and suddenly I realize she might've incited a fetish I never knew I had. Maybe it's not so new, it's just everything about her is tempting.

She claims real estate on the couch corner while I grab a bottle of Chablis from the wine fridge under the kitchen counter. And after carefully placing the glasses of wine on the table, I sit on the opposite end of the couch, with a good two feet of cushions between us. The lights are dim and the fire in the hearth illuminates the room with a soft glow. The atmosphere is romantic, intimate. But my libido is racing like a bullet train. So, I need to remind myself to keep my distance or else this train will make a detour toward her tunnel.

"If you suggest we should watch a sappy movie because I'm a girl, I'll cut your balls off, Martin."

Fuck, this girl, I'll gladly hand over my balls. "I don't doubt that you would do that, Dee."

Her bright smile lightens up the whole room.

"Smart man," she says as she takes the remote from the table in front of us and starts jumping between channels until she finds a Keanu Reeves movie about a chain smoker with the ability to perceive angels and demons on the human plane.

She looks over at me and simply states, "We're watching this, so don't even start saying this movie is a flop." I find myself smiling, waiting for whatever crazy rant is about to come out of her mouth. "It made more than two hundred million at the box office and earned itself a bit of a cult following after its release. And Keanu is a god."

"I'm not saying a word. I wouldn't dare stand between a girl and her dark-haired celebrity crush…" Before I have the chance to finish the sentence, a cushion hits my head.

"Jerk," Destinee menacingly calls me while still smiling.

"Well, this jerk was thinking about making the new Matrix movie a huge event with a big screen on the terrace. Snacks, drinks, the fire pit… but since you're insulting me so vehemently, I should exclude you from my guest list."

Dee gives me a deadly glare, but her luscious lips are tipping up. "You're worse than I'd imagined."

"You have no idea." My admission is so honest, and at the same time, it hides so much. If she only knew the thoughts that are running through my mind right now.

And it has nothing to do with mortals fighting angels and demons. Or jumping from a window in a mental hospital. But I gotta admit it has a lot to do with insanity.

Gabriel, God's messenger, plays a huge role in the plot of the movie. She's intrigued, so she asks, "Do you think your parents wanted to name the four of you after the archangels?"

"Says the girl who was named after destiny?"

"You got me there," she chuckles. "But tell me anyway."

"Destinee, you knew us as kids. We weren't exactly angels."

"Your older brother is a gentleman," she says without looking at me. "Erin is a lucky girl. And someday you'll find someone, and you'll make her just as happy."

I clear my throat, it suddenly feels oddly tight. "I'm not looking for the one." Because she's in front of me right now.

The movie plot thickens, and she pays attention to the screen as if it were the first time she's watching it.

And my eyes are fixed on her. On the curve of her slender neck. Her new hairstyle and the way her hands flex when Constantine transports himself to the inferno looking for a girl who committed suicide.

"I feel like I'm a bit like Isabel," Dee says, talking about the suicidal girl.

"What do you mean?" I reply with a frown. Is she struggling with her mental health?

"I'm not thinking of taking my own life. No need to frown at me, mister," she scolds me, her blue gaze, clouded by pain, roams over the room, avoiding my stare. "The thing is, I also ran away from my issues. I left my family confused and my best friend when she needed me the most. All of them know me well. They know I've always wanted to live close to home, and see... here I am now, hiding like a coward."

"Hey," I reach for her hand and take it between mine. Our fingers entwine and electricity sparks between the two of us. She also feels it, I can tell by the way her spine straightens and her breathing changes. "Listen to me. You did what you needed to survive. There is nothing to feel ashamed of, Destinee. You're starting a new chapter in your life."

Her blue eyes are shining, filled with questions.

"You think I'll be able to?" she asks with a shyness I've never seen in her before. And I don't like it.

If David broke her spirit, I'll be here to help her to get her strength back.

"Dee, you are only able to transform your destiny if you transform yourself first. You're changing your life… taking the reins. You're doing what nobody else can do for you."

"Don't you think I'm running away?"

"Dee, the pain is inside you. You can't run away from that. But you can learn how to deal with it. If you need a fresh start to do it, then go for it."

The pain vanishes from the deep sea of her eyes. And then something happens.

Something magical and unexpected.

Destinee leans against me, her small hands resting on my legs while she comes closer, and closer, until her lips touch the corner of my mouth and kisses me softly.

My hands are fists at the sides of my body. It takes all my strength not to pull her against me and devour her as she deserves to be kissed. Deeply.

What was I thinking when I invited her to stay here with me tonight?

This is gonna be a long night.

# CHAPTER FIVE

*Destinee*

What in the living hell possessed me to kiss Martin that way?

Have I lost my freaking mind?

With the way Martin is looking at me, it's as if he were certain I have lost my sanity.

Just when I'm ready to flee in panic, his hands tighten over mine that are still on his strong legs, keeping me in place.

"Dee," my name on his lips sounds like a warning. And a plea.

An explosion resounds from the sound system, making me jump. We both turn to the screen for a beat before I'm the sole focus of his attention once again.

"Hey," he whispers, his brown eyes burning with so much heat. "It's just us, ok?"

Four simple words, and at the same time they are filled with so much meaning. Martin is right, this is us. The girl who used to run with her hair in pigtails around their orchard and the boy who always carried me on his shoulders when I was too tired to walk.

"Look," I say, pointing with my chin to the television. I can't bear his intense stare on me for another second. It's like he's trying to strip me down. No, I'm not talking about my body but my very soul. "He's going to heaven."

I love the movie. I know this could put me in the weirdo zone for thinking the whole plot is about sacrifice and selflessness, but I really don't care.

"You're such a dork," he attempts to pull me back into his side by taking my hand, but I hit him with a throw pillow using my free hand.

"Says the boy who always tried to make me laugh by telling bad math jokes."

"Hey, the oven one was good!" There's no use, Martin is the worst comedian *ever*. Good thing he made a fortune putting his beloved numbers together.

"Ok, whatever you say. Why did the mathematician spill all of his food in the oven? Because the directions said, 'Put it in the oven at one hundred and eighty degrees.'" I snort. "Yeah, a classic."

"You laughed, I remember that well," he says indignantly.

"Yes, I cracked up because you were so ridiculous."

Martin places his hands over his heart as if he were in pain. This is us, as he said. I know his old tricks. "You wound me, Destinee."

"Just your pride. You'll survive," I reply prissily, and then pat his cheek. His stubble prickles my palm, igniting something inside me, making me ask questions I really shouldn't. *How would it feel against my thighs? Or my bare tits? Grazing down my neck?*

But the scariest thing is, why am I having all these thoughts about him?

"Want more wine?" Thank you, Martin for getting me out of my head. At least, that's one I can answer with ease.

"Yes, please." I can manage more wine, but when he stands and walks to the kitchen my eyes are glued to the way those dark jeans fit his fine ass.

I'm on a direct flight to hell.

And Constantine won't be there to save me.

"Want some popcorn?"

"Only if you have M&M's to mix with it."

"You're so weird," he chuckles.

"You like me anyway," I sass back.

"True." A single word, and it carries so much more meaning.

What's happening here?

Where's this magic feeling coming from?

Why *him*?

While the corn pops in the microwave, I have a mini panic attack. But it gives me time to get myself together. When Martin comes back with a bowl full of popcorn and a bag of milk chocolate M&M's, I've got my emotions in check.

"What do you want to watch now?" he asks me, pointing to the remote on the couch.

"Nothing," I reply. "Let's talk. Tell me everything about your work. What new app are you developing these days, my genius friend?"

Martin gives me a small smile. "Do you really wanna know?"

I shrug before answering, "Of course. I'm asking you, right?"

"A couple of weeks ago, a girl from San Diego contacted me. She developed an algorithm for a dating app. The idea alone is smart, but her interface needed work." My hands move, inviting him to keep talking. "That's one of our strongest points. All our apps are user-friendly."

I understand what he's talking about. In the end, it doesn't matter what you do, seeing your client, user, or patient, as a real person, does the trick.

And dating is scary enough, no one wants to read instructions like those that come with furniture you need to assemble.

"Will you be traveling south often?" I have no right. It isn't my place to question, yet still…

Martin studies me before replying, "The girl is really quirky. We just talk over the phone, and we're working together online a lot. But I don't even know what she looks like."

A pang of jealousy rushes over me. My brain can't understand the reason, but it's there. "And you're intrigued?"

"I'm human," he replies as if that was enough of a response. "I'm curious about her, for sure. But there is nothing beyond that."

A hum of satisfaction leaves my chest. "Tell me more."

"Well, we are doing research for our own apps. Two games, and one application, that with some luck, we could sell to the health department."

"That sounds interesting."

"It was inspired by my mother," he says softly, and my heart feels heavy for him. I know how much they all loved Mrs. Posada, and how devastated they were when she passed away. "The plan is to collect all the information, past medications, everything in one place. Like a big hub. This would help patients get the best medical attention quickly."

This is right up my alley.

"I love it. I'll help you in any way I can."

"Quit your job and come work with us?"

"You want me at your beck and call, Posada?"

Again, there is so much heat in those gorgeous brown eyes. "You have no idea."

Gah, he's so flirty, and charming. And so freaking handsome.

Curling my fist in the bowl I fill my mouth with popcorn and chocolate before I say something stupid. Or worse, really kiss him this time.

*Stupid, horny girl. He's your ex's brother. You shouldn't be imagining those Kamasutra-worthy images with him…*

Martin keeps talking, while we laugh and make light conversation.

We continue on like this until a yawn escapes me.

"That's our cue. Time for bed." *Are you coming with me?* My mind is filled with thoughts of us in it. Naked and sweaty. I should get outta here and never look back.

*Get it together tonight, Destinee. Tomorrow you'll go back to the safety of your own home and Martin Posada will be just a memory. A very nice memory, indeed.*

"Let me grab some stuff from the bedroom and I'll be out of your hair."

While he rushes to the room, I decide to play a little joke on him. Grabbing one throw blanket, and making myself comfortable on the couch, I close my eyes. When his strong steps sound out on the hardwood flooring, I close my eyes and let out a loud snore.

I can feel him hovering over me. Then I let out another snore. I want to bite my lips because…

"Are you summoning your inner bear or what?"

And I lose it… I'm in stitches, laughing so hard fat tears roll down my cheeks.

It's so easy to be around him. It's confusing and at the same time, my soul feels like he's the much-needed rain in a barren desert. He's soothing my pain. But I fear if we let this escalate, the disaster would reach epic proportions.

After I gather myself, he guides me to his room.

"Sleep tight, *cariño,*" he says before kissing my forehead and heading out of his bedroom. I know what that word means. It's like love but in a caring way.

I love it, and at the same time, it's a reminder I'm just like another little sister to him.

A man like him would never look at a girl like me as anything more.

I'm beyond the friend zone. I'm firmly parked in Sisterland, being with him would be so wrong. The question is, why does it feel so right?

The sound of my phone ringing on the bedside table awakens me. Who the hell is calling this early on a Saturday?

I pick up the call without paying much attention to the caller ID, just wanting the noise to stop drilling into my head.

"Hey, babe." Fuck, that voice… talk about drilling.

"I'm hanging up."

"No, Dee, give me a minute," David, my ex, pleads. "I'm in Sunnyville," he announces with too much joy for my delicate state.

"Good for you," I reply, my voice full of bitterness. I couldn't care less about his whereabouts.

"I came to visit my father," he adds.

"Lucky for him," I know firsthand how much Mr. Posada loves his boys.

"I want to see you." Hell no!

"I don't think that's a good idea."

"Dee, please. I really want to see you."

"Such a pity. I'm not available."

I hear a groan coming from the other side of the line. This is a classic example of David's behavior. He just wants to see me when it's easy and convenient. He never made a real effort for me. How was I so stupid to accept that? My only excuse is love is blind. Or maybe it was just an addiction, I was a junkie for him.

"Babe, please… Let me in, I'm outside your door." A straight fact, he wants a quickie before visiting his father… the poor delusional guy.

"No, David. We are done for real. Keep pounding on the door, I'm sure the new tenant will call the police in no time."

"Destinee... open up!" His voice is joined with a strong knock.

This whole conversation is pissing me off. I need to get rid of this guy right the fuck now!

How did I manage to have a relationship with him for the past eleven years—on and off—is a mystery to me. Don't you dare judge me.

"Now you're ready to beg for forgiveness, David. Did you forget that time I realized I was your side dish? Or the fact you just used me for sex? Oh, let's not forget the time when you left me alone when I needed you the most."

I hear him sigh. "We need to talk, Dee. You know how much you mean to me, babe. We have history, don't throw it away."

I roll my eyes. I know he can't see me, but still. David is simply exasperating. "I'm not home. I moved. I'm living far away from you, don't make me change my number too."

He gasps. "You moved out of Sunnyville?"

See, unbelievable, right? I did it anyway.

"Yes!"

"Dee, you're kidding me."

"Goodbye, David. Have a good life."

And I press the red icon on my screen, feeling pleased with myself. David isn't used to the word no, let alone coming out of my mouth. But the sooner he realizes he will be hearing it a lot, the better.

My chest feels heavy, as if I just finished running a marathon. My breathing is short and fast. Fucking David.

A soft knock on the door calls to my attention. "Can I come in?"

"Sure," I reply without a care in the world.

"Breakfast is ready," Martin says while entering the room.

He looks so yummy at this time of day, even better than last night. He's wearing joggers, an old t-shirt, and a smile just for me.

"Are you ok?"

No, I'm not ok. But suddenly, it seems like the world is spinning in the right direction again.

The sky's the limit, right?

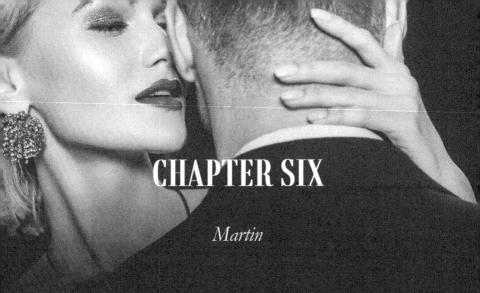

# CHAPTER SIX

*Martin*

What the hell am I doing listening to her conversation with my brother behind the door like a fucking stalker?

She's on the phone, speaking to my brother. Actually more like, asking him to go and fuck himself.

A strange sensation of pride fills the space between my ribs, but my brain decided today to be a twatwaffle and register a different message than the one's earlier. Destinee Carr is off-limits, you dickhead. Recalling the words of Blaise Pascal, the mathematician, "The heart has its reasons which reason knows nothing of…" The meaning hitting me hard like an avalanche. I'm sure the old fellow was involved in a shitty situation like this one, loving someone from afar.

Destinee ends the call and growls. My first instinct is to go to her and let her know she's not alone. Before I can stop myself, my knuckles are rapping against the door.

"Breakfast is ready," I say in a way of a greeting, just to test the waters.

At the sight of her in my bed, my heart starts to beat faster. She managed to capture the moonlight inside her, and now it's shining between my gray sheets.

"Are you ok?" My feet are rooted at the side of the bed, waiting for her to give me something.

She looks at the ceiling for a minute as if the crystal of the light fixture were interesting. Then her silvery-blue eyes are back on me. Electrifying my body, making me weak.

"Your brother called. He wanted to see me."

David doesn't deserve her, the idiot never gave her what she really needed: love, care, his undivided attention.

His time.

"And what did you say?" I'm playing dumb here. As if I didn't hear her side of the conversation.

"He's in Sunnyville visiting your father, and well… he wanted to *see* me," she says while looking at the French doors at the other side of the room. "He was pounding at my door, ready for me to cave in."

My eyes roll almost involuntarily. This is so David. Always looking for the easy way, how he manages to keep a job—as good as the one he has—is still a mystery to me.

"What did you say?"

"I told him that I'm sure the new tenant isn't going to be happy about the disturbance and I'm sure they'd call the police if he keeps pounding on the door."

Well, I'm positive that's not the pounding my brother had in mind… but he made his bed—a cold solitary one. And now he'll lie there—by himself.

"Okay. Well," I start, ready to change the direction of the conversation and the entire mood. Destinee's with me, and this is the first time I have her all to myself. I want this day to be memorable. "Everything is ready for breakfast. Are you hungry?"

Her beautiful face lights up after hearing my words. "I'm always ready to eat."

Then she jumps out of bed and runs to the bathroom. "What did you fix for us?"

That makes me smile. Broadly. This girl. "Well, why don't you hurry up and find out for yourself."

"What time did you wake up this morning to make all this stuff?" Destinee asks me before taking a huge bite of her barbacoa taco.

We're sitting at my breakfast bar, next to each other. Eating and talking, and having fun as if we do this often. I wish. She's still wearing the same t-shirt she slept in last night and put on one of my gym shorts, looking so fucking beautiful it hurts.

I sip my coffee and stare into her gorgeous eyes. "If I had made all of this myself, I probably wouldn't have slept a wink at all."

She pouts. Her rosy lips are calling my name. My control is wavering every time I take a glance, a temptation too great for a guy to resist. "Now I don't feel special anymore."

Dee has no idea how special she really is to me. It's beyond her wildest imagination, that's for sure.

"You should still feel special. Maybe I didn't cook all of this, but I heated it up for us… and believe me, I don't share my favorite dishes with just anybody."

On the marble counter, there is a Mexican buffet laid out just for the two of us.

She speaks with a mouth full of food. "I need you to tell me where to find this because it's gonna be my new favorite restaurant."

"I think I'll keep that secret to myself," I counter. "If you want more, you'll have to come back here."

"You have me hooked, like a junkie, Martin."

"And I'm your dealer," I reply smugly. "You want more… you know where to find it."

I like to cook, but as my schedule is so busy, it's hard to find the time to do it daily. But a couple of years ago, one of my employees told me about his mother's home catering business. Since then, I've been her best client. Twice a week,

Marietta delivers enough food to feed a small army directly to my door.

Refried beans, hand-made flour tortillas, whatever you want. The woman cooks like a pro that can fill anyone up, of any size. I'm a big boy that needs a lot of fuel.

"What are your plans for today?"

She shrugs and then answers, "You know, the typical Saturday in the life of any single girl. Cleaning, laundry, cooking my meals for the week... I'm living my best life, as you can see."

"Stay here with me."

Her eyes are as round as saucers. "Martin, I can't," I hear her whisper.

"Why not?" I'm ready to do whatever I need to if she stays with me. Forever. "Because you have laundry and I have a perfectly functional washer here. Stay, I promise we'll have a great time."

A flame of interest sparks in those eyes. "What do you have in mind?"

"It's a surprise!"

"You're full of them, aren't you?"

"Oh, baby, you have no idea." Truer words have never been spoken.

"I need to go home. To take a shower, change my clothes... and grab my hamper. You offered your washer, and don't think for a hot minute I won't take advantage of that. I hate going to the laundromat."

Damn, this woman. She captivates me with every word leaving her lips like no other woman before. With every smile. With every beautiful hair on her head. She is perfect… and she was meant to be mine.

"Want to take a shower while I clean up?" I ask her.

"It should be me doing that," she replies.

"What kind of host would I be then if I made you do that?" There is no way I would leave her here to do all the clean up by herself while I relax in the shower. "Let me show you where the towels are."

"Why are you doing this for me, Martin?"

"Because I want to," I tell her and start walking to my bedroom without looking back while she's still processing my words.

I want her, not just because she's here. Not because she's single. Or even because she's within reach.

I want her for the woman she is and always has been. But mainly because I need her, she's the one—my one.

Forgoing the shower at my place, she changes back into the clothes from the night before while taking one of my sweaters. She decided that she needed to go home first so she could shower there and grab her things. Destinee lives in a pool house in the back of a huge property with tall privacy walls and a gated entryway. The place is small and a bit outdated. The carpet is faded at the corners, and maybe the kitchen requires newer appliances, but it's clean and cozy.

"Don't judge the place by its décor," she warns me. "I rented the place furnished."

I smile, taking a look at the small couch in the room's corner. There is a coffee table painted in a glossy shade of pink.

"I didn't say anything. But, what's that smell?"

"Lavender," Dee replies. "This place was so musty because it was vacant for way too long. So, I had to do something to get rid of scent."

"Yeah, it's probably been empty since Reagan was in office."

"Don't be a dick," Destinee scolds me.

"Now you wanna talk about my dick? Sure, it's big. You wanna peek?"

I'm rewarded with a roll of her beautiful eyes.

"I'm gonna take a shower. Sit and wait for me, I'll be quick." She starts walking to her bedroom door then stops in her tracks. "Don't do anything to make me regret my choice, ok?"

I smile and do as I was told until I hear the sound of the shower running. Then I'm a man on a mission. I check the locks, the windows, her car's tires, oil—and just about everything concerning her safety. I know from experience that Destinee likes to take her sweet time getting ready, so I have about an hour to accomplish all the tasks.

After I'm satisfied with the results, I go back to park my ass in the place she designated so she'd be none the wiser of my actions. I'm replying to some emails when a text from my older brother comes in.

**Gabriel:** Erin is busy with wedding stuff, up for a beer?

**Martin:** Sorry, bro. Busy today.

If he only knew what my plans for the day are.

**Gabriel:** This is part of your best man duties. Working overtime doesn't count as plans for a Saturday, *hermano*.

Gabriel knows me well, he knows that's my usual M.O. on the weekend. But he isn't aware of the interruption to my regularly scheduled program.

**Martin:** I'm not at the office.

**Gabriel:** Perfect, I'll pick you up in twenty.

**Martin:** I'm not at home either.

**Gabriel:** Where the heck are you?

I'm surprised he hasn't called me by now. Gabriel is the typical big brother, but on steroids. He's bossy, protective, used to snapping his fingers and having his younger brothers comply…

**Martin:** I'm with Destinee.

Of course, my phone starts ringing with these three words.

"Excuse me? Can you repeat that?" Gabriel hisses.

"I'm with Destinee."

"In Sunnyville? What are you doing there? Dad said David is visiting him today. My guess is you both didn't drive into town together."

I take a deep breath before replying. "I'm not in Sunnyville. Destinee lives here… in Silicon Valley."

"What?"

My brother knows the predicament I'm in, so I tell him everything that has happened since Dee and I ran into each other at the bar.

"Haven't you talked to Elena lately?" I ask him.

"When I try to talk to her, she always wants to speak to Erin—not me. They're both on a mission, to make this wedding as big and luxurious as they can."

"You're so whipped," I tell him and I hear him chuckle down the line.

"And you're walking a dangerous path, Tin." Every time he calls me by my childhood nickname, I'm brought back to a time when I tried to imitate whatever my older brother did.

At this point in my life, more than thirty years later, the feeling is still there. I want what my brother has. He's not only successful as a businessman, but he figured out his personal life. Gabriel found an amazing girl, and they're getting married in a couple of months.

No, it isn't envy. Nor jealousy. It's more like a yearning. Yearning for the girl on the other side of the door.

"Five more minutes," I hear Destinee shout through the door. Infamous words, I have at least a half an hour more to finish the conversation with my brother before she is done.

"Martin," my brother says. I'm sure he heard Destinee's voice. "You know I'm on your side, but this shit is like walking through a minefield. Do you even know if she feels something for you? Five minutes ago, she was in love with David."

"I know," I reply in a low voice. "That's the reason I want to spend time with her."

"Destinee is a special girl, Martin," he says. "Just be careful, ok? Don't get hurt."

"I won't," I lie to him, but more so, to myself. I know this will hurt in some way but I'm ready to take a leap of faith, it doesn't matter if I break both my legs and my heart with the fall. She's more than worth it.

"I'm ready." Destinee comes into view, and my mouth gets dry.

She looks amazing.

"Gotta go," I say on the phone, ending the call. My gaze transfixed on the girl in front of me.

My brother screams something about calling him later, but I don't give a fuck. Not when Destinee stands before me in a crop top along with jeans, which shows a strip of skin that teases me. It shows just enough to make me drool and get hard. But she soon covers herself up with my sweater again.

It doesn't matter, I'll still have to contend with my boner all day long, knowing she's wearing my clothing.

# CHAPTER SEVEN

## *Destinee*

This is electrifying, this feeling.

This sensation is one I've never experienced before today.

Every time I turn my head, his eyes are on me. Especially when his large sweater keeps falling from my shoulder, his gaze follows the path of the fabric. I feel empowered... yet terrified. There is this new dynamic between us, the tenderness in his voice when he speaks to me. His eagerness to make this weekend memorable. The last few hours have been like opening the doors to a whole new world I didn't know existed.

I like my body—most of the time. I've learned to embrace my flaws and enhance my assets. In high school, I was the last of my friends to blossom. So when my boobs finally started to develop, I was more than ready to showcase them. I haven't stopped since then. I'm the kind of woman who knows what to wear that's flattering. But today, everything is different.

It took me forever to decide, I stood in front of my closet for a long time. I wanted something pretty but I didn't want it to seem like I was trying too hard. Don't ask me why. I wish I knew the answer. As I just said, everything is different with him.

Martin and I are drinking hot chocolate perched on stools on a rooftop café in a building I'm pretty sure isn't open to the general public. It seems the man is a king around here. At least four people have stopped by to say hi since we entered the premises.

We visited a little shed where Silicon Valley was born. Martin gave me the most entertaining history lesson. Even for a man who speaks the number's language, it was fun and engaging. He explained how the first company product, an audio oscillator was built in that very same place from tools that to me look foreign.

"All of this happened thanks to the Dean of the Engineering department," he added. "The man encourages his students to open their electronics company here in the area instead of leaving the state."

"But why California?" I asked, curious about the subject. To this day, Silicon Valley contributes millions to the US GDP. And living here is expensive, hence why I was only able to afford the little pool house I'm living in at the moment. The area is consistently ranked as one of the most expensive places to live in the entire country.

He replies while smiling at my curiosity. "The Bay Area had long been a major site for research and technology. Even in war times, there was a lot happening here, then the transistor revolution came, and the rest is history."

"Why did you go for mathematics instead of engineering or computer science?"

He shrugs before replying, "I like numbers. In the end, they are the foundation to make the rest of the equation possible."

I remember going to his college graduation. Of course, I was busy with David the entire time, but images of him in his robe looking so proud of what he accomplished while his mother fussed around him taking a thousand pictures is imprinted in my memories.

And at the same moment, a different image takes over. Me standing at his side, his strong arms on my waist while he smiled and kissed me. What if I had fallen in love with the other brother? What would Martin have thought of a teenage girl having a crush on him? I always thought he had a soft spot for me until he went to college. That summer—I started dating David—everything changed.

It doesn't matter, the 'if only' doesn't exist, anyway.

After discussing the pros and cons of the area development, he took me to the Android Lawn and waited patiently, laughing at my shenanigans while I photographed myself with every statue around the park.

At some point, he pulled his phone out of his pocket and took a selfie of us together. Secretly, I wish I had the chance to save more memories of us forever. I want to burn every image in my mind, the way his jeans cling to his narrow hips and how the corners of his eyes wrinkle every time he smiles at me.

"Why didn't we do this before?" I ask after sipping more hot chocolate. It's delicious, with cinnamon, just the way I like it.

"What do you mean?"

"Talk," I reply nonchalantly. "I've missed you, Martin. Remember when we used to spend time together… alone. And unafraid."

Something passes quickly through his gorgeous brown eyes. Was it sadness?

"Because you were always focused on other things."

Yeah, his brother.

"But even if I was at your parents' home, you left every time," I continue, searching for more answers. "If for any reason we were alone in the kitchen or running around the orchard, you left immediately. As if I had a contagious disease."

He looks directly into my eyes but remains silent for a couple of moments. Then turns to look at the people gathering around.

"There is a lot you don't know," he finally replies without looking at me.

"Did something happen with David?"

"Maybe I'll tell you one day. I don't know." Martin bends one of his legs leaning over the stool, his boot-clad feet dangling.

"Why don't you tell me now?" I push him to respond. "If you were upset because of me... I'm sorry, Martin, I really am."

I lean over to touch his arm with my hand, but he moves as if my contact will burn him.

"It was more than that," he says, cryptically.

"Are you sure you don't want to tell me now?"

"Yes." he replies. The word said in that careful and reserved tone sounds like a warning. He seems almost angry... at the situation or me, I don't know?

Bravo, Destinee, way to kill the moment.

"Hey," I whisper. This time trying to be conciliatory, reaching the same point where we were just minutes ago. "Take me home if you're tired, ok? I had a wonderful time and..."

Martin reaches for my hand and pulls me toward his muscular chest. My hands landing on the hard planes of his pecs.

"You have nothing to be sorry about," he says. This time his brown gaze is seeking mine filled with sincerity and contrition. "I'm just being an idiot." As he kisses my head.

Martin might be admitting to being an idiot, but it sure feels like it's me now, because I have no idea what's happening here.

"Are you sure everything is fine?"

"It is now," he murmurs and then gives me another kiss, this time on my forehead.

Why do his hands, his lips, his eyes on me feel perfect?

"Are you hungry? I know of a place you might like."

"I'm always hungry," I give him my answer and a little smile. "Don't you know me by now?"

He smiles from ear to ear before saying, "I do."

"I need to make a quick trip to the ladies' room…"

"I'll be here waiting."

With unsteady legs, I walk to the restroom and take care of my business as fast as I can. I look at my reflection in the mirror. I don't recognize the girl standing before me, she's smiling, her eyes sparkling and full of possibilities. Drying my hands, I almost run back to where Martin is waiting for me when I stop in my tracks. He isn't alone anymore.

Fuck.

There is a tall, willowy young blonde woman telling him something. He smiles while she moves her hands and both of them laugh. Then she leans in and whispers something to him. She's clearly flirting. Suddenly, I'm regretting my decision to cut my long blonde mane.

I know the moves. The way she's looking at him through her lashes and moves her hair over a shoulder. For a moment, her face looks a bit familiar, where have I seen her before? She's standing tall, showcasing her assets. Well, there isn't much to show, she's tall and lean. Model type. Is she his type?

A pang of jealousy runs through me like an electric charge, leaving me more confused than before. When the bitch touches his arm, my vision turns red. I'm ready to rip her arm off and declare war.

Without thinking about my next move, I find myself walking toward them.

There is such a thing as women peeing around their men to keep the hoes at bay?

Martin smiles and takes my hand. "Here she is," he announces.

"Hi," I smile, but it doesn't reach my eyes. My gaze roaming over the other girl, telling her without words to back the fuck off.

"Valeska was asking me about the Stanford tour," he says. "I was giving her some pointers."

"Yes, pointers. Sure!"

In a strange accent, she cuts in, "He's a local."

Yeah, bitch. I know. You weren't looking for pointers, more like a rod to ride all the way to Stanford and back—his rod to be specific. Keep your paws away, he's mine.

Wait, what? Thinking about it surprises me... however...

"What's the best place to have dinner? My friends and I want to go out later, and maybe for drinks after... if you... both of you, of course, want to join us."

This time I responded before he could. "We made plans, then we're heading back home."

I let the word home sound like more, like I'm staying at his apartment forever.

Martin just smiles, as I continue. "I'm sure you can find a great place to eat if you check out Yelp."

There, I can speak her language. If she's here, it's because the woman is some kind of computer or internet geek so she should know how to use an app.

"We're featuring the place in our next video," she adds with a touch of smugness in her voice.

"She's TikTok famous," Martin clarifies when he notices I have no idea what she's talking about.

"Oh, I see." And that, ladies and gentlemen, is the reason her face looks familiar. The woman, Valeska Pence is one of the biggest stars of said app. "I thought your team did some research or something."

"I like to try new things every now and then," she adds in a sultry voice but to me, it sounds like nails on a chalkboard.

"Why don't you jump directly into the unknown?" I say in a fake sugary sweet voice, and I swear Martin is chuckling.

The fucker. Of course, as every red-blooded man, loves a good cat fight.

"You know what? Maybe I will." Then her hand lands on Martin's thigh. "See you soon, Martin. You know where to find me."

"Yeah, in your next fifteen second video."

My stare follows her while she walks away, the whole time I feel eyes on me.

"That was fun," he finally breaks the silence.

"For you, maybe," I reply, acid pouring from my tone.

"You don't have a single reason to be jealous."

His words hit me like a ton of bricks. Hard reality check. He's not mine… we're only spending the weekend together. I'm just a family friend. That's it, that's all.

"I know."

"Destinee…" he pleads. "Look at me."

I refuse, I refuse to let him know I'm hurting. He isn't the one to blame for my ugly scars, the same marks I hide from the rest of the world.

"Destinee." he says my name again, this time joined by his hand on my waist.

I love the feel of his hand on me.

"I've been here before, you know?" I mutter. "To all of you, I was David's girl. But here, when he was in the city, I was just another notch on his bedpost."

I swear I can hear Martin's teeth grinding.

"I promised myself I would never be put in that position again. I really want to change my life for good. I want it all, Martin. The white picket fence with kids and a dog. If I can't find the man who checks all my boxes, I'll do it alone. I've worked my ass off, and in a few years, I'll afford to have a nicer place for me and a baby. I deserve it."

I'm sure he thinks I'm running on baby fever after seeing his sister being so happy.

"You know what?" he tells me, his arm around me tightening.

"What?"

"Nothing is impossible for the ones who believe," he encourages me. "Just don't stop believing, Dee. If that's what you want, I'm sure you'll get it. Sooner rather than later."

For some reason, he makes me believe every single word he says. He has spoken with so much conviction, as if he were dealing with the universe itself to conspire in my favor.

"Now, let's get you fed," he stands, taking me with him. "You're getting hangry."

# CHAPTER EIGHT

*Martin*

I take Destinee to a restaurant I've been to before on business. Yes, I love the food here but today is different because she's by my side, which makes the whole occasion memorable.

The dim yellow lights create the perfect ambiance, with bistro tables spread throughout the room, which has wall-to-wall hardwood flooring. At night the atmosphere in the restaurant is romantic, perfect for seduction. I'm a man on a mission. I didn't bring Destinee here with the goal to fuck her tonight. I'm laying the foundation to woo her and show her my love for a chance at forever. As a mathematician, I understand that a child isn't ready to figure out long complicated equations. It takes time and skill to learn how to solve each one and what method you should use for it. I've been waiting for years for Destinee, a few weeks or even months more mean nothing if in the end she's with me. No great thing is created suddenly, a philosopher once said, right?

"What do you call a mathematician who spent all summer at the beach?" Dee says after the waiter walks away with our orders.

She claims I'm *the bad comedian here?*

She's so freaking cute, I hear myself asking, "I don't know, what?"

"A tan-gent." Then she snorts out a laugh.

"Good thing you're a nurse," I give her a smirk.

The place is filled with loud conversations and laughter, the movement at a nearby table calls our attention. The waiter carries a small cake on a dish toward a couple and a minute after he places it on their table, the man at the table goes down on bended knee in front of his woman. Asking her to marry him. When she responds with an obvious yes, the whole place erupts in applause but my gaze is on Dee.

Instead of this superficial small talk, I want to ask real questions and get answers that reach deep into the heart of her. My gut is screaming to ask her why she was so upset in the coffee shop earlier when the woman Valeska came over to talk to me. Yes, she was flirting, but there was distance between us at all times. I know how to deal with women like her, I'm not a teenage boy after all. I'm a grown-ass man.

With her silvery blue eyes still on the couple, they're full of tears, something inside me simmers with need. When was the last time I got laid? But the mere idea of being with another woman repulses me. It has to be her.

"I don't have a ring in my pocket today, if you're wondering," I tell her, trying to make a joke.

And she rewards me with the stink eye. "Don't spoil the moment," she chastises me. "It was beautiful."

"One day you will be there, Dee. In that position, looking at the love of your life kneeling in front of you."

She gives me a sad smile. "I'd like to know where my better half is. Or if he even exists."

"You're sorely mistaken there, Dee," I correct her. "You're the better half. If the fucker doesn't realize that, then he doesn't deserve you."

This time her smile reaches those gorgeous pale blue eyes. "I'm really enjoying my time with you, Martin Posada."

"I'm really enjoying my time with you, too, Destinee Carr." And I intend to spend all my days with you. I just need to convince you somehow.

"Do you remember the time you tried to make me wear those ridiculous overalls to go fishing?"

I do, that was the last time I took her with me to the creek. A week after that was my eighteenth birthday, and following my mother's advice, I took a step back. She said it was too creepy for an adult man to wander around the orchard with a preteen girl. Even if she was like a sister to me back then. We weren't related, so I did as my mom advised.

"And you ended up drenched anyway," I laugh.

"Because you carried me over your shoulder and tossed me into the water!"

"Our recollections may vary, Ms. Carr."

She's telling the truth. I was bragging about my muscles and showing her how strong I was. Destinee was furious with me afterward and swore she wouldn't talk to me again in her whole life. Her ridiculous threat only lasted twenty minutes, Destinee is a chatterbox. Silence wasn't made for her.

When the food comes, the subject changes to my family's upcoming events. Gabriel's wedding in Lake Tahoe and the arrival of Elena's baby.

"I bet it's a girl. Cardan will be over the moon, and your father…"

"Both of them are waiting for a little Lena to spoil."

"Do you want kids someday?" she asks me, her eyes sparkling like the *mousseux* she's sipping.

"Absolutely," I reply with the truth.

"Aren't you one of those mysterious millionaires with skeletons in the closet and a kinky taste for sex?"

How much champagne has she drank tonight?

With her mention of sex, I can't help picturing her under me. And on top. Stretched out on my desk…

Discreetly, I adjust my pants before replying, thinking about my preferences with her looking at me with raptured interest ignites something in me. "Are you curious about what I like in bed, Dee?"

Red blooms across her cheeks. "I just want to get to know you better," she replies, looking at the lamb shank on the plate in front of her.

"Then just ask me."

"You never told me if you want kids."

"Are you offering to be the mother of my offspring?"

"You're exasperating," she complains. "Just answer me, no more games."

She has very little idea what kind of games I'd like to play with her. Playing naked would be my choice.

And somewhere more private, preferably.

Her gaze looks directly into mine, her sculpted eyebrows lift, urging me to respond.

"I do," I finally answer. "I want kids. Several of them."

"Enough for a soccer team?"

I ponder for a moment. "No, I still want alone time with my wife. Two or three would be amazing."

"You plan to get married soon?"

"It depends on…" I leave the other part of my answer unspoken.

"Whoever she is, will be a lucky girl," she adds. Yearning stains her words.

"I'll be a happy bastard when I get her."

"What kind of girl are you looking for?"

You. I want to say. I bite my tongue to stay silent for a minute while searching for the right words that she's ready to accept at this moment without running away.

"Smart, funny, family-orientated, pretty much someone who's ready to deal with my boisterous family."

"Not a supermodel you can parade on your arm?" *Oh, cariño... I'd be proud to have you at my side any time if you let me.*

"It's more than just looks, Destinee," I say, my gaze on hers, she needs to understand what I mean. "Her true beauty will reside beneath her scars."

She clears her throat. "What else?" her voice is just a whisper.

"I want her to be open with me," I start testing the waters. "Adventurous, ready to accept whatever I provide her—in and out of the bedroom."

Another blush stains her face. *Are you feeling the heat between us, Destinee?*

"Tell me something no one else knows about you." She's getting more daring and I love it. The restaurant and all the voices around us vanish, we are in our own private world.

"I will as long as you do the same. I want to know a secret about you."

She nods in agreement, waiting for my reply.

"I've learned to live with one regret," I muster up. "I'm working on moving beyond it but it isn't easy."

"What do you regret?"

"That's two questions," I counterargue. "An answer for an answer, *cariño*. That was our deal."

"I lied," she whispers and takes a sip of her champagne before talking again. "Every time I told Elena about my Tinder dates, I lied."

"What do you mean?"

"That's another question? You aren't playing fair, too, Martin."

"My biggest regret is wasting too much time being a fucking coward. A chicken shit man incapable of going after what he wanted—still wants—the most."

This is my one regret. However, that's in the past, I'm looking forward to the future… one with her in it.

I'm ready to fight for her. To win her over. My war isn't against David, but the pain he left her to bear. To battle against her own fears.

She looks at me open-mouthed, until she replies, "I never went on those dates. I just bragged about my sexcapades to your sister. About all those men I met and never actually fooled around with. But I felt I had to lie, it seemed pathetic of me to be pining after David while he continued on with his life happily." Then she takes a long pause after her confession. I have no words because I'm solely thinking about all the ways to beat my brother to a pulp'.

No woman deserves this. Dee doesn't deserve this.

My father taught us to be honorable men and David was a prick.

"Thinking back on our relationship now makes me feel so weak," she pauses and cracks another sad smile. *Fucking David.* "Near the end something happened that made me realize enough is enough. I wasted too many years waiting for him to change… to love me back."

"I do think David loved you in his own way." Why the hell am I defending him? I want to smack my own head.

"It wasn't enough, Martin. I want to live my life with a man who's ready to love me in the way I deserve. Without boundaries, without fear."

I do. I want to scream. I really do.

"But first there is a lot I need to work on, you know. My self-love, my inner strength."

"You're stronger than you give yourself credit for, Dee." I don't give a fuck if this sounds cheesy. "You lost your way in the fog, *cariño.* But you're finding your way back and I know you will end up in a beautiful place. Don't be ashamed of your past. That's what makes you the wonderful woman you are now."

She looks at me. Fuck, those eyes will be the death of me. My weakness.

"You know what? When you put it that way, I believe it. You make me feel strong, Martin. With you I feel beautiful."

Fuck it, I need to touch her. Leaning over the white linen of the tablecloth, I reach for her hand and take it in mine.

"You are," I assure her. "Just own it, Dee."

The waiter chooses this moment to interrupt. "How is everything this evening?"

"Everything is good," Dee replies, but her eyes are still on mine.

"Is there anything else I can get you?"

"Coffee for me, another glass of champagne for the lady. And the dessert menu."

"Right away, sir," the waiter says and walks away.

"That's too much, Martin. I shouldn't drink anymore."

"Just one more glass," I say. "We're celebrating tonight."

"What exactly are we celebrating? I thought we celebrated my first week at work more than enough last night."

I smile at her, even if my body is craving for me to take those rosy lips and kiss her passionately. "No, baby. We're celebrating new beginnings."

We take our time to leave the restaurant, but afterwards we take a stroll with no destination in mind. Dee's hands are on my arm, her curves leaning on my flank, it feels so good. It's like subconsciously her body was looking for warmth in mine, I'm fine with that. But my mind is working overtime with its own agenda. Picturing us tucked together in my bed, her head on my shoulder. Her entire body relaxed and sated. Destinee in my arms, the arms that will hold her forever. Her hands on my chest, the chest of a man whose heart beats just for her. I'll show her dreams can come true. I'll show her what love really feels like.

"These booties are killing me," she says after a while.

I take a look at her boot-clad feet. Those things can't be comfortable, and it has been a long day.

"Don't look at my shoes that way," she chastises me. "This girl likes her heels. She needs to take whatever opportunity she has to wear them because she only wears sensible shoes at work."

"You're funny when you talk about yourself in third person. You're so weird."

"You like me anyway, dork."

"I do," I reply. "Let's take you home before you get blisters."

Then her forehead wrinkles as she recalls and cries out, "Ah shit, I just remembered that a hamper full of dirty clothing is waiting for me at your place."

"You want to watch another movie while we wait for your laundry?" My lips tip up with amusement.

"Nah," she says. "I'll do it in the morning after another night in your bed."

Too bad I won't be in there with her, I'm looking forward to the day when we can finally share it.

# CHAPTER NINE

## *Destinee*

"Don't be ridiculous, there's enough room for both of us," I tell him while he looks at me as if I sprouted another head. "We are doing this my way, or not at all."

"We shouldn't," he replies as if I were asking him to swim with the sharks.

"It's not that hard, Martin." I attempt to convince him. "I promise you'll be in one piece afterward."

His eyes are as dark as the coffee I like to drink in the mornings when he mutters, "The couch isn't that bad. I slept on it last night."

My eyebrows lift dubiously. "So you can hate me in the morning when you wake up sore. Since this is my second night here at your insistence and—"

Martin makes a sound of amusement as he cuts me off. "Says the girl who declared she'll be moving in."

I feel the heat creeping up my neck, but I lift my chin in a stubborn gesture, anyway. "I was joking, Martin. You know what a joke is, right?"

"Were you?" Now he's biting his lip, as if he were trying to stifle a laugh.

"I told you I'm a great comedian."

"Of course," he replies, his voice full of mischief.

"Then it's settled," I announced, picking up one of the pillows and throwing it on the other side of the bed. "You're sleeping here with me tonight."

"I really shouldn't," he mutters stubbornly, but out of the corner of my eye I can see him eyeing the mattress.

"Ok, I'm not gonna force you." I know with my next statement that I'll win this silly argument. "I'll see you later, I'm gonna call an Uber to pick me up." For the added effect, I begin walking toward my purse.

His expression changes instantly. "You aren't going anywhere," he declares while grasping my wrist lightly, the touch sends a charge of electricity I feel in every cell of my body.

If something like this happened with David, he would let me go without a second thought. Whereas Martin doesn't want me to leave, and he makes me feel so secure and wanted. Allowing me to stay in his bed all cozy while he sleeps alone and uncomfortable on the couch.

Both of us freeze at our contact. Whatever I'm feeling I know he's feeling it as well.

He clears his throat and speaks first. "I mean, it's late and it has been a long day."

"You're tired. I'm tired. Your bed is big enough for the both of us and a football team…"

His dark eyes shine with mischief. "Are you planning a gangbang?"

"Yeah." I go with the flow. "I'm calling all my peeps right now. Three is enough for you?"

"Are you planning to walk in the morning?"

Damn this man is cocky.

"Oh no, friend," I pause to inform him. "All those are for you!"

For a moment, it's like time stands still. The next thing I know, I'm on the bed with at least one hundred and eighty pounds of man pinning me down, both my wrists trapped with one of his long hands while the other tickles me relentlessly.

"Stop, please. Or I'm gonna pee on your fancy mattress," I plead for mercy. He gives me no reprieve and when the stubble on his chin grazes my arm, I'm a goner.

A moan escapes from my mouth, I'm not laughing anymore. My entire body is on fire, I'm so turned on. Turned on by *him*.

Oh God. With how I'm feeling, I guarantee Satan is waiting for me in hell. He's probably laughing his ass off at the moment. The man looming over me is everything I want. He occupies all of my senses. The sight of his deep brown eyes on mine, hypnotizing. The delicious smell of his cologne in my lungs, enticing. His name on my lips tastes sweet, mouthwatering. All my breath in sync with his is the only sound I can hear, harmoniously. And his touch, it's magical, mesmerizing. All these feelings combined are unbelievably overwhelming. I'm under his spell and I don't want to be released... ever.

I swear the hard ridge of an erection is poking against my hip... what's happening here? Is Martin aroused—by *me?*

"Martin," his name on my lips is a plea. However, I'm not sure who's taking the lead here. If it's my hormones or my brain.

My feelings are more than tangible now, with the touch of his short beard and the warmth of his wet tongue on my skin. My being is simmering, this is the most erotic moment of my life and I'm still completely clothed. Here with Martin, who I've known all my life but I'm beginning to see him in a new light.

Why is something that should be wrong, feel so freaking right?

Somehow, it's like he's rearranging all of my broken pieces. Filling the spaces with his attention, with me being his sole focus. It's the most wonderful thing, being held with so much consideration. Making my heart beat in a new rhythm. Staining my soul with new memories. Trumpets begin blaring out of nowhere. Don't tell me that the four horsemen of the Apocalypse are here to get me.

"Fuck, it's my father," Martin says, untangling his body from mine. "I need to take this."

Phew, that's a relief. I give him a short nod while he stands and grabs his phone from the nightstand.

"Hey, *viejo,*" he says tenderly on the phone. I've heard this greeting at least ten thousand times. "Is everything okay?"

There's a silence while he listens to Mr. Posada talking, his face turning pale.

"I'll pick you up in the morning. I have contacts at the Stanford Hospital," Martin states. "I'll get you the best care."

His entire demeanor has changed. He's now sitting up on the side of the bed, his elbows resting on his thighs. His head bowed down while the phone is firmly against his ear, listening intently. I can see he's fighting to stay in control of his own emotions.

"You can't ask that of me, *papá.* Of course I'm going to worry, you're all I have left."

My hand lands on his shoulders in comfort before I can do anything to stop myself. Martin leans into my touch like a wounded animal.

"I know you won't live forever…" A bitter laugh escapes him. "I just…"

Martin closes his eyes while I caress the strong line of his jaw. Everything about him is enthralling, even the stubble peppering his skin.

"I'll be there in the morning, ok?" Leaving no room for argument. "I'll call Lena now… see you tomorrow."

"*Sí, papá*, see you soon. Yes, I'll be careful. No, I won't take the bike. Don't worry about me."

Then he ends the call and stays silent for a couple of minutes.

"My father fell today. He was at Lena and Cardan's helping them paint the nursery…"

"Did they take him to the ER?"

"Yes," he replies. "The doctor said it was something with his sugar levels. They sent him home…"

Sunnyville Memorial Hospital is a good place to be treated. Mr. Posada would've been in good hands.

"That's good news, I'm sure if the emergency doctor had some concerns, he would have ordered him to stay at least the night at the hospital."

"Why didn't my sister call me?"

The reason is more than evident to me. "I'm sure your father asked her not to."

"I'm going to see him tomorrow. You're more than welcome to stay here while I'm away... I just... I just need to be there."

My heart clenches for him. The Posadas are a tight bunch.

"My father hasn't been the same since my mother's been gone. What if..."

No, no. We aren't going there. Martin's father is as strong as an ox, he'll be fine.

"You want me to go with you?"

His eyes open in shock. "Would you?"

"Of course. You know your dad is like a father to me. Plus, that will give me the chance to see my mother and show her that I'm still in one piece."

In an instant, his arms are around me. "Thank you." He kisses the side of my head with so much need and tenderness. It feels like I'm the air he needs to breathe. His lifeline.

He pulls back to look at me. "Hey," he whispers. "I'm sure all my brothers will be there tomorrow. I'd understand if you..."

"Don't worry about me," I give him a smile even if my heart is beating hard against my ribs. "I'm a big girl. Sooner or later, I'll have to see David."

"That's my girl." I'm rewarded with another one of his tight hugs. His heart is beating fast, the steady sound is comforting and arousing at the same time. "Let's get your laundry done. We're leaving early."

His phone starts ringing again and our bubble bursts for a second time.

"It's about time," Martin snaps on the phone. I'm sure Elena is on the other end. "What happened?"

I'm sure Lena is recounting the same story his father just told.

"Yeah, your call is a little late," he scolds his sister. "Yeah, I know."

Martin laughs at whatever she says.

"She didn't have my number. We just met by chance in a bar on Friday night." I listen while Martin gives Elena a brief rundown of our encounter. "I invited her to have dinner with me tonight. Yes, she's with me now. We're heading there together in the morning."

Good thing he doesn't say a word about me staying here—in his bed. To be honest, I wouldn't know how to explain this to my best friend. Whatever is happening here feels too new and fragile. And I guess the first step is to talk… maybe I'm taking this the wrong way. Perhaps, he's just being friendly, and my heart is listening to whatever it wants.

"Yes," his hand is softly touching my knee. "Hang on… Lena wants to talk with you."

"Hey, bitch," I greet my bestie.

"Hey," she offers back. "Seems like fate played better than any of my schemes."

"You're a wacko. What schemes?"

"Erin and I planned to send Ruben or Martin to your new place to help you move."

This girl is crazy. "I moved ten days ago, Elena. All my stuff is organized already."

"Anyway," she says, dismissing me. "I planned to do something for you, but there's so much to do here. The baby is almost due, and I swear I have' mommy-brain. Some days I barely remember my name."

"You better remember mine, because I'll be the godmother."

"Of course you will," she says. "See you in the morning, ok? I'll have breakfast ready for you guys."

"See you then."

After ending the call, we start my laundry lost in our own thoughts. I'm busy separating whites and colors while Martin watches me silently leaning against the doorjamb.

When the washing machine is full and the cycle starts, he takes my hand and guides me to his terrace. The night is chilly, but soon I feel the warmth of his chest to my back while we quietly watch the city lights and the stars above us.

"Martin."

"Mm-hmm." I can feel his breath caressing my neck.

"Am I dreaming?" This feels like a fantasy, too good to be true.

"If you are, please don't wake up."

"What's happening here?" I ask, trembling. "Between us?"

"Everything is happening." He turns me in his arms. Our gazes meet and I understand what he's saying.

Yes. Everything is happening.

My life won't be the same after him.

# CHAPTER TEN

*Martin*

I should tell her.

Fuck, I'm gonna tell her.

But I don't think Destinee is' ready to hear what I have to say. Her eyes full of tears hide nothing. With this girl, what you see is what you get.

"Dee, I can wait until you're ready."

We are so close I can feel her breath whisper across my lips. I long to kiss her. Clutching to the last threads of my self-control, I force myself to step back so we can talk.

"Why would you do that?"

"Because I've been waiting for years. My patience is limitless when it comes to you." It really isn't but I'm determined to see it through as long as we end up together—if it's even possible.

I feel her spine stiffen at the shock of my declaration. It would be too much for anybody. "Martin… I…"

"I know, *cariño.*" I say, my voice soft and comforting while I continue to caress her. "You aren't ready, yet. You came here to start over and here I am, like a *cabrón,* putting you in an impossible situation."

Yes, I realize I'm being an ass because I know this is not the right time.

Her hands on my chest tremble.

"What do you want, Destinee? What do you really want?" After hearing my question, her eyes widen in disbelief. You can tell that she isn't used to being asked about her wishes. I want to throttle my brother for how he treated her.

Dee doesn't reply right away, she takes some time to choose her words wisely. With her unwavering gaze she finally speaks, "I want to be happy. I want to discover who I really am. I want to be loved, but more than that, I want to love myself. Maybe I'm being a selfish bitch, but that's what I really want."

"Hey." I tighten my grasp around her. "You're not being selfish. You deserve all that and more. You are a strong woman, who's decided to take control of her life and live it to the fullest."

A tear rolls down her cheek and I hurry to wipe it away with my thumb. "I feel stupid. For fuck's sake, I'm a soon-to-be twenty-eight-year-old woman who hasn't figured her life out."

I'm drowning in the deep blue of her eyes. "Well… I'm a soon-to-be thirty-three-year-old man who has been pining over a girl from afar for years wishing she was his."

"I don't want to talk about our past right now," she says softly, her caress is like a feather across my jaw. "Running into you yesterday, opened my eyes to new possibilities…"

I can't help but smile. "Tell me more."

"What do you want to know?" she asks. "My friend was telling me about the hottie who was staring at me and…"

"You were by far the most beautiful woman in the place."

"Just in the place? You wound me, Martin," she attempts to lighten the mood.

"You know I've always liked your long hair," I tell her while running my fingers through some strands. "But this cut looks killer on you. I couldn't take my eyes off you the entire night."

"How do you think I felt? You walking toward me looking so hot and perfect with your short beard, your strong arms, and that sexy smile."

"I wanted you that night—I still want you," I confess in a low voice.

"I'm so confused," she admits. "We spent so much time together growing up. But after a while you put distance between the two of us. I felt like you abandoned me. But now you're here. I missed my friend. I missed *you.*"

*Mierda.* Yeah, shit.

"I had to," I explain what my mother suggested and then my decision to stay away when she started a relationship with my brother. "I had to, it hurt too much."

"I'm sorry."

"You have nothing to apologize for, Dee. It wasn't our time." The weight of my own words hits me hard. "And now it is?"

"It'll be when you're ready, *cariño.*"

"I'm torn," she says. "A part of me needs space to heal by myself, and the other wants to stay here with you. In your home, laughing, talking, and watching movies. I just want to be with you."

"Do you still want to come with me tomorrow?"

Destinee pats my chest with her open hand. "Your family is important to you, as is mine. That's the way it should be."

"I hate to cut this short, baby," I say even if I don't want to. "But we are leaving early in the morning. We should go check on your laundry and see if it's done."

Her forehead drops to my chest, and she giggles. "Reality sucks."

"We'll make it work, somehow," I assure her, but I'm betting that it'll be more than a bit complicated.

"How?"

"You said you wanted to spend time with me. Just the both of us doing everyday stuff. Let's do that and see where it goes. Allow me to take you out and walk you to your door. I'll buy you flowers just because. This gives me a chance to get to know the woman you've become."

"I don't understand why you would do all of this."

I can't hold back anymore. I kiss her. Then, with her taste in my mouth, I say, "Because you're worth it."

I pull her back into my embrace.

"Let's finish with the laundry. We need to sleep, tomorrow will be a long day."

Sleeping with her in my bed is glorious torture.

That's what this is. Looking at her beautiful face with her warm body in my arms is too much. She's too close. I'm supposed to be a man with limitless self-control.

It's a struggle. But I'm doing it for her.

Her round ass pressed to the ridge of my erection is beyond tempting. Even deep in slumber, Destinee's body seeks out mine. It's better than I've ever imagined and believe me, I've dreamt about something like this plenty. Although in my fantasies, we weren't wearing a single stitch of clothing while my hands wander to all her secret places.

Before bed I put on pajama pants and a t-shirt while she emerged from the bathroom in flannel pants and a tank top. Sans bra. Those pert nipples were hard and screaming for attention. Her outfit is not something I'd normally consider sexy, but on her, she got me more than aroused. Somehow during the night I managed to behave like a gentleman. This morning is a different story though… My body is in need of release. My mind knows better than to push. So that my soul won't lose its better half.

Beyond the window the sun starts rising, inching into the darkness of the room. It's still too early to wake her up, but I really should untangle my body from hers. Maybe, go for a run to burn off some of this tension, but I find myself unable to do it.

I close my eyes allowing my imagination to run wild. Fantasizing about the moment when my fingers could slip into her warm and welcoming pussy. Destinee shifts her body more, which makes her sweet ass rub against my already aching cock.

"That thing in your pants can't be comfortable," I hear her saying in a raspy voice.

I swear she knows what she's doing. She moves again but I move quickly to stop her.

"Destinee." I warn her. My voice is heavy with desire. Full of want. "I thought we're taking this slow."

She doesn't take my warning seriously and keeps going. Fuck.

"I want to see you come undone," she whispers.

"So your goal is to make me come in my pants like a teenager. Have I got that right?"

"Yeah."

"Keep wiggling that sweet ass of yours like that and we'll soon find out."

Her back arches and she surprises me by taking my hand, guiding it down the waist of her pants and the cotton of her panties. My fingers burn from the heat of her.

Destinee wants me to join in and play. Game fucking on! We'll both be coming out on top.

I kiss the side of her soft neck, the satiny skin of her shoulder while whispering words in Spanish she won't understand but I know she'll feel. I tell her how beautiful she is, how much she means to me, how honored I am by her trust. My mouth is revving her up while my fingers are taking control of her wet pussy. Kissing and stroking. Getting her ready to take off and soar. She's so fucking receptive to my touch, as if she were made just for me—my pleasure.

Although what we have is forbidden, the one thing I'm absolutely sure of... is that I need her. Her body. Her heart. Her soul. Just. Her.

Dee's walls tighten around my fingers, she's so close, and I'm dying to feel her coming. If I could, I would give up

113

my career and do this all day long. Nothing would give me more pleasure than hearing her sweet mouth scream my name in rapture.

"Oh my God," she gasps.

"It's just me, *cariño,*" I joke. "But you're allowed to call me whatever you want."

"Keep touching me like that and…"

She doesn't have the chance to utter another word while her entire body convulses in pleasure. Destinee's ass over the ridge of my cock is driving me crazy, I feel my body tensing, as a tingle travels up my spine. She bites into my arm attempting to muffle her moans of ecstasy. A battle scar I will proudly wear.

We fall over the edge in tandem. It's downright amazing how in sync we are. I want more moments like this forever.

"Good morning," she says in a mellow, sated voice.

I kiss the soft spot behind her ear. Good morning indeed.

# CHAPTER ELEVEN

*Destinee*

Everything has changed and now I don't know how to feel about it.

A part of me is thrilled. Fueled by excitement and ready to discover what fate has in store for me. For us. But this annoying little voice in my head hasn't stopped screaming that something is going to go terribly wrong.

Now that the adrenaline rush has passed with reality rushing back. I wonder if I will be able to leave this bed. Not because my body isn't working. But my mind is in overdrive. I feel terribly shy… yeah, shy with the man who made me see stars. With the man who's kissing my shoulder as if I were the most delicious thing he ever tasted.

I want his fingers between my folds again, making me forget. Making me feel like I'm whole. Like I'm enough.

"I need a shower," he whispers in my ear. I know what this means, he's inviting me to join him. I snuggle deeper into the blankets. "Come with me," Martin finally says, noticing I'm not moving.

"What time is it?" Sun rays are peeking outside. I'm sure there's still time to be lazy, even for a little bit. And a breather is required on my part.

"Just past six," he replies.

"Too early," I excuse myself. "I need five more minutes."

"Dee…" he murmurs. My name on his lips sounds like he's trying to bring down the weak defenses I'm trying to build back up.

"I need time, ok?"

He says nothing more, just kisses my shoulder again and goes to the en-suite bathroom. When he closes the door, I can feel hot tears streaming down my cheeks. I close my eyes feeling weak and small. Tired as if I were running for miles.

I take another pillow, this one smells like him. I hug it tighter. On the other side of the door is a man who wants to be with me, to take me out, and buy me flowers. I remember all his words from last night. And here I am wallowing in my self-pity, feeling like I don't deserve any of that.

What in the living hell is wrong with me?

The delectable aroma of his cologne comes in waves, even before he utters a word. I close my eyes tighter, hiding my tears from him. I'm sure it isn't working, but after a tense silence he finally says, "I'll make coffee."

The sound of his footsteps announces he left. Making me feel even worse. I have no idea how much time has passed by the time I venture to the bathroom. The stream of warm water is so welcomed. With my loofah I scrub my skin hard, as if that would take all the shame out of me.

From the hamper filled to the brim with now clean clothing, I take a set of blue sweats, socks, and my practical cotton underwear. Dressed and ready to go, I venture to the kitchen. Wearing my cozy outfit like armor.

As I walk around, I find the space empty. Maybe he decided to go to his office? Somehow, I'm sure he wouldn't leave without telling me. I smile at the thought. The coffee maker is full of hot java and beside it there is a mug with a jar of cream and the sugar bowl.

I turn to the window after fixing myself a cup, my fingers curling around the warm ceramic. Martin is there, walking around with the phone next to his ear talking. He's dressed in gray sweatpants, a matching sweatshirt, and a black jacket. His feet clad in clean white sneakers. I can't help but to observe that the man looks lickable from head to toe.

There is no other cup in the sink, so I hurry to get one ready for him. I have no idea how he takes his, but I bet he takes it black. He's still on the phone when I walk toward him with the steaming cup in my hand.

"I have no idea what that means," I hear him saying. "You tell me. Seems like you have everything figured out."

Then he laughs, as he listens to whatever his interlocutor says.

"Yeah," Martin adds. "I'm just waiting for Dee to get ready, then we'll be on our way."

He pauses to listen.

"See you in a while, Gabriel."

The two of them are so close. Brothers and best friends. I remember his mother telling me about how Martin was born just ten months after Gabriel. I love how he uses the Spanish pronunciation for his brother's name, making it sound so strong. It's something the Posada siblings do all the time. I've never attempted, though.

"Hey," I greet him, closing the distance between us, while fighting with my insecurities to seem as normal as possible. "Want some?"

His intense brown gaze narrows on me, studying me. Then he takes his cup from my hand, and mine as well. Setting them both on a teak wood table.

"Everything good?" he asks me. With the way he's looking at me, I know he's expecting an honest answer.

One I'm incapable of delivering.

"Yeah," I reply with a shrug.

"Then…" he says but his words die the moment his lips touch mine. A soft and gentle sweep, enough that I can taste his minty breath. The kiss is soft but I feel it strongly as if the floor beneath my feet has vanished.

His strong hands hold the sides of my face captive, keeping me in place, where he wants me. The rough pad of his thumb draws a line on my lip, following it like a trail with his lips. The tenderness of the kiss is tearing me down, making me lightheaded and weak in the knees.

I lean forward, begging him to kiss me harder. But he doesn't and just carries on with his languid pace. Brick by brick my defenses fall. As do my doubts.

I can let my guard down. Around him, I feel safe.

He begins to deepen the kiss, consuming me with unbridled hunger. Finally, my arms are looped around his neck, my fingers locked between the strands of his thick, raven hair.

Yes, this is exactly what I needed. His mouth devouring mine, while his arms tighten around me where I don't know where I end and he begins.

Never before have I been kissed this way, I feel it down to my very soul. This type of kiss would rival the ones I'd find in the romance novels I like to read. He tips my head back, running his tongue along the curve of my neck, up to my ear. Nudging me closer to the cliff. This man could easily make me fall… in love. Hard and fast.

I can feel his cock hardening between us. All I want is for him to tear off all my clothes and take me back to bed. Or wherever we can have some privacy. I want to grant him access to do all the things he wants to me.

When I think he's ready for more, he lets out a ragged breath. "Are you ready?"

Huh? Ready for what?

He chuckles at my confusion. The dickhead knows what he's doing to me.

"Gabriel called. They're leaving now. We should do the same, *cariño,*" he reminds me while touching my face softly.

Right. We're visiting his family today. His father is sick.

The sun is shining high above us, but the breeze is cold. I don't want to leave the warm shelter of his arms. But real life waits for no one. Not everything is about you, Destinee. Stop being a selfish bitch.

"Are you sure you need all that stuff," Martin asks me, noticing I'm packing all my clothing.

I glance over at him.

"Tomorrow is Monday, I have to go to work," I retort. "Not all of us are millionaires… I'm on payroll."

"I have to work too," he replies, taking the hamper from my hands. "I want you here anyway."

"Martin, I love your bed and your bathroom. But I have my own place, remember?"

He says something about dreams that last forever. Why do those words sound so familiar?

In the garage, with a hand on the small of my back, he guides me to a shiny black Jeep.

"This way, *cariño*," he says while opening the trunk door and placing my things there.

"I see you're trading the eco-friendly car for a gas-guzzler."

He winks at me. "This one is a hybrid."

Martin makes sure I'm safely in my seat before walking around the car to take his place. After one more earth-shattering kiss, we're on our way. The car is the definition of luxury; all leather and polished wood with a huge screen behind the wheel. It may be luxurious, but it's still practical and comfortable enough for a long road trip.

While Martin drives and the distance closes, my nerves start to spike.

This won't be the first time we see each other after our breakup. We were on and off throughout our eleven years together. We broke up at least twenty times, but this time there's no going back. I deserve better.

I'm not giving up my lifelong friendship with Elena just because her brother is a prick. We promised each other years ago, no matter what, we would be friends forever. I intend to keep my word.

"Everything will be fine," Martin reassures me as if he knows what's running through my mind. "I'll be there with you the whole time."

"I know." Even though I know it's impossible for me to hide behind him at every moment. My big girl panties are firmly in place and I intend to stay away from David as much as I can.

"Want something to eat?"

"Are you nuts?" I laugh a little. "Knowing your sister, she started cooking last night driving Cardan crazy. I know for a fact that there'll be enough food to feed a small army as soon as we arrive."

He says nothing, but smiles and takes a pair of aviator glasses from the dashboard.

It takes us almost two hours to arrive at La Gloria, the Posadas' orchard, even with the weekend traffic. Elena and their father own the orchard, since the boys decided they didn't have any interest in running it. Lena loves living here, and she knows everything about mangoes. Plus, she and her husband just built a gorgeous farmhouse north of the property.

Martin is parking his Jeep beside Gabriel's sleek sedan, when the house door opens, and Elena comes running out. Well, as much as her pregnant bump allows. Cardan at her heels.

"You're here," Elena says while hugging me.

That makes me laugh. "You, weirdo. It's only been two weeks."

"It feels like an eon," she replies. "You left at the worst time ever. The baby will be here anytime soon…"

"Elena, that's still four months away…"

"Time flies, my friend…" she starts babbling about the nursery so fast I can barely catch a word. "Erin is inside with Gabriel. We were waiting for you to eat. But I'm hungry…"

"Uh-oh… hangry pregnant woman alert."

"She's angry all the time," her husband comments.

"Or horny," she adds.

"I don't want to know about it," Martin grumbles from behind us. "Cardan, you can tell me about the garage and this app you want to develop to track your clients…"

"You guys are such nerds," Elena says, rolling her brown eyes. "Erin brought some samples with her and we want you to see them before deciding."

Wait a second, we were talking about the nursery, then the food… What' are we talking about now?

Ignacio—Mr. Posada—comes to greet us at the door followed by Erin and Gabriel. After a round of hugs, we all sit around the kitchen table.

"Let's eat. Ruben and David will arrive in the afternoon," says Mr. Posada, placing a huge tureen at the middle of the table. "Ruben had an event last night and they're driving in together."

"Is this what I think it is?"

"Yes," Elena replies proudly. "I made pork pozole just for you."

"Aw, Lena, I love you."

"What about the rest of us?" Gabriel deadpans, but a smile is pulling his mouth up.

I lift the lid to discover the red Mexican soup I love so much. With lots of white corn, the dish is served with cabbage and radish. It's a bit spicy, but utterly delicious.

Martin is seated beside me, I want to intertwine my hand with his, but somehow restrain myself.

Mr. Posada seems as well as ever, but as soon as we finish with breakfast, I want to have a discussion with him, and take a look at his test results if he has them.

I'm sprinkling my soup with oregano leaves when the front door opens and a voice I know so well calls out loud.

"Familia, we're home!"

I can feel my body tensing immediately.

He's here.

Shit.

# CHAPTER TWELVE

*Martin*

I love that she's here with me, sitting at my family's kitchen table. But there's distance between us. I can't kiss her openly like I want to. Fuck, she's mine now, and I want the entire world to know it.

I look at my brother and his fiancée. Then I look at my sister and her husband. Fuck. I want what they have. I want to be able to throw my arm on the back of her chair while we talk and laugh with my family. I want it all with her.

Dee stretches over the table to grab the little bowl where my sister has placed the oregano. It takes all my control to not put my hands on her as she's bent over. I'm drowning in lust.

"Familia, we're home!" My brother shouts while entering the house. I feel the tension taking over her body, mine reacts in the same way. But the worst thing is knowing I can't do anything, not yet.

I'd tell my own brother to fuck off if she'd allow me to.

Gabriel, the only one who knows what's happening, shoots me a warning look and stands to greet our younger brothers. Ruben enters first, hugging our father and then kissing the girls' cheeks. He sits beside Destinee and starts talking with her while David talks with my father and takes the chair beside Cardan on the other side of the table. David does all this without taking his eyes off her. This fucker has some gall.

"You got here early," my father says to Ruben.

"The event last night was so boring I went home before nine. It seemed like a good idea to make the drive earlier than we planned."

"Fancy seeing you here," David says looking at Destinee, who tenses again. "Seems like you were lying when you said you moved."

I can feel Gabriel's eyes on me, as if my brother were trying to hold me in place.

"Oh, I did move," Dee says, her pained gaze on him. "But Lena called me last night, so here I am."

"Where are you living now? Sacramento?"

"None of your business," she replies firmly, then turns to speak to my father. "Mr. Posada, I'd like to read your results, if that's possible, before I go visit my family. I'm sure you're fine, but I know your family would feel better if I explain things in a language they'd understand."

"*Papá,* please," Lena pleads before my father has the chance to refuse. "We all trust Destinee."

"Speak for yourself," David disagrees.

"David Alejandro!" my father reprimands him. We are all grown men now, but in this family when my father talks, we listen.

"I'm sorry," he mumbles.

"Ok, don't do it again. Destinee is like family to us and I'm thankful she spared the time to be here today."

After my father's firm statement, David lifts his spoon to his mouth, in an attempt to stay silent, no doubt. I know him, he wants to grab her by the arm and take her to a private place so he can feed her more lies and have his way with her again.

"Oh," says Erin with more excitement than needed. "The ties we ordered arrived last week. The colors are so perfect."

This girl is a saint. Not only does she deal with Gabriel's shit everyday, but by how she changes the subject and moves the conversation to lighter topics.

"We're going for our suit fittings the week before Christmas," Gabriel reminds us, as if he didn't send us a detailed email with the wedding itinerary. This wedding planning turns chicks crazy. I wonder how Destinee would be?

Gabriel and Erin decided they aren't having a wedding party. But for aesthetic purposes, all the men in our family are wearing the same shade of blue suits paired with white bespoke shirts and burgundy colored ties.

We finish our meal and as we've done since we were kids, it's up to the men to pick up everything and help clean the kitchen. Gabriel and I are on dish duty while David and Ruben wipe down the counters and pack up the leftovers. Destinee, Erin, Elena, and my father stay seated around the table while Cardan makes coffee.

"Let's go to my office," I hear my father saying. It's about time we discuss the reason why we're all here. We do check in regularly, but when one of us needs help, we're there; the Posada family is as tight as vines especially since my mother passed away and with Elena's news. As soon as my father and Destinee leave the room, David says, "I can't believe she's here, of all places. I've been looking for her everywhere."

My back tenses up, and again I force myself to remain as cool as a cucumber.

"You're a little late, fucker, you already messed up too many times," Ruben adds. Yep, like ten years too late. David was such a prick to her.

"She's talking to me today. She has no choice but to listen," David states as if it were a fact.

Then Gabriel says, "A woman always has the choice, *hermanito*. You would only have half the problems you have the moment you understand that."

"Says the man who went after his girl like a derailed train," David jokes.

Gabriel looks at him with narrowed eyes. "I was determined to make her mine, truly mine. But I've always honored Erin's wishes. It doesn't matter if we're married or not. She comes first."

"I'm sure she does," Ruben snickers.

"Fucker," Gabriel says. "I'm being serious, David. Let her go, you wasted your chance."

"Several of them," I hear myself saying the words before I can stop them.

"How is that any of your business?" David turns to confront me.

"*Papá* told you why," I tell him. "Destinee is like family to us."

Way more than that to me, but I bite my tongue.

David's gaze narrows on me. "You think I don't know, motherfucker?"

"What are you talking about?" Gabriel asks and at the same time David takes two steps forward, standing almost in front of me, ready to fight.

"This fucker has been in love with her since forever," David replies.

"That isn't true," Gabriel answers for me.

"Why isn't he denying it then?"

"Because it doesn't matter," Gabriel interjects again. "Martin has nothing to do with the fact that you screwed it up, David."

"And now he's ready to screw her, right?" David replies sardonically.

"Don't fucking talk about her that way." Anger evident in each word I speak.

"See?" David says while patting my chest hard. "He's ready to fight for her. To put her over his own blood."

"I think it means more than just blood, bro," Cardan says. "It's more about respect. What would you do if we were talking about Elena, instead of Destinee?"

A chorus of 'cut your balls,' 'hit the shit out of you,' and 'cut your dick off' is heard in the kitchen.

Cardan smiles before adding, "Gabriel is right, David. You should let Destinee go. I'm sure you'll find a girl to have fun with, in no time. Just be honest with her, that's it."

Elena and Erin are sitting around the table, looking at us in stunned silence. I'm sure Lena is dying to give us a piece of her mind, but somehow, she remains silent.

"We came here today to see *papá* and see what our options are," Ruben says in interruption. "Not to brawl between us and stress him the fuck out."

"The doctor says he's fine, tired but fine. They just need to run some more tests. Yesterday, his blood pressure and sugar levels were within the normal range," Cardan informs us.

"Why the dizziness, then?" I ask out loud.

"Your father has been so stubborn about working with Elena and I in our new backyard… he's probably just tired."

"I'm taking him home with me," I say immediately. "First thing tomorrow morning, I'll get my assistant to find the best internist to treat him."

"Why don't we all calm down and see what Destinee has to say?" Elena says from the place beside the window.

"Destinee isn't a doctor," David says. He doesn't even respect the fact she earned her title.

"She's a nurse practitioner," I add.

"Since when do you know so much about my girl?"

"She's not your girl anymore," I remind my brother. "And I listen to her, more than that, I see her worth."

"You talk like a pussy-whipped motherfucker." David comes at me again, and when he moves to push me, Cardan stands between us.

"Go outside and calm the fuck down. Don't come back until you have." My tone brooks no argument, I don't care what he thinks about me, but David needs to learn how to respect Destinee, and our father's wishes.

"And since when are you the boss around here?"

"Stop acting like a spoiled brat," Gabriel blurts out. "Go outside and take a breather, before I kick your ass."

"As if you could," David says, but walks toward the kitchen door and leaves before slamming it closed with a loud bang.

"What the fuck is going on?" Ruben asks after a minute of tense silence.

"Your brother is acting like an asshole," Cardan replies.

"Is what he said true, Martin," Lena stands, walking toward us. "You're in love with Dee?"

Her eyes are full of concern. I hate myself for creating this mess, but not for how I feel about Destinee.

"I…" I begin.

"Ok, everything is fine," Dee says, coming into the kitchen with my father in tow.

"What's with the long faces?" she asks, her voice full of concern.

"Just waiting for you guys," I say, walking toward my father. I place one of my hands on his shoulder. Is he skinnier than the last time I was here? "You scared us, *viejo.*"

My father, *mi papá*. I hope I'm half the man he is when I get to his age.

"I'm fine," he sighs. "Please tell my kids, Destinee."

"He is," she replies with a little smile. "But he also needs to take it easy and go for those tests the doctor ordered."

"Ok, that's good," Elena says.

"He can continue working with Cardan in the yard, just taking more breaks and hydrating himself. Plus, I think Mr. Posada needs to sleep better. I'm sure his doctor will talk with you all about that." Destinee continues to explain.

"You aren't sleeping well, *papá?*" Even if the answer scares me, I ask.

"I just miss my wife." His voice breaks. *Mierda,* this is hard for all of us, but everything pales in comparison to the fact he lost the love of his life and is still mourning her.

My eyes water, I loved my mother and still miss her every single day. Sometimes I find' myself with the phone in my hand ready to dial her number.

"Who wants to see the nursery?" Elena chirps, casting a light in the fog of sadness engulfing us.

"I'm in," Erin lifts her hand.

"I need to grab my charger from the car, I'll be right back," says Dee. I'm sure she's looking for an excuse to have a moment to collect herself.

When the girls leave, I turn toward the fridge. Looking for anything. I'd prefer something strong to drink, a whisky, but at this time of the day, some water will have to do.

"It's always a joy to have all my boys at home," my father says. "Where is David?"

"Taking a call," Ruben lies.

Minutes pass, and Destinee hasn't come back. My gut tells me something is wrong and I need to act. Now.

# CHAPTER THIRTEEN

*Destinee*

I take a moment to myself. Seeing David was a shock, but not in the way I had thought. It was more like, 'ok, I'm here at your family home and I don't want to weep because you left me when I needed you the most.' It was more like, 'fuck off, I can live without you.'

I found my strength again, I just needed that little push to find it in the place that it was hidden so many years ago.

Taking the phone from the pocket of my sweatpants, I make the call I've been dreading for the last couple of weeks.

"Hey, Mom," I say on the phone after she answers on the second ring.

"Baby girl! Are you ok? Do you need me to send your father to the police station? He can be there in no time if he leaves now…"

"Mom, I'm not at the police station," I tell her. "I'm actually at the Posadas' orchard. I asked Martin to drive me to see you in a bit."

"We're having breakfast with your aunt Daisy in Petaluma."

Just my luck, this happens when you want to surprise your parents. Mine are always busy. I roll my eyes.

"Too bad you're missing the chance to see for yourself that I'm still in one piece."

"Are you brushing your hair? Eating all your greens? I know how demanding that job of yours can be."

"I'm fine, Mom." I say rolling my eyes once again.

"You're coming for Thanksgiving, right?"

"Am I still invited?"

"Don't be so dramatic, Destinee Dalilah. We'll be here waiting for you."

I ponder that for a moment. In our family, the leftover Black Friday breakfast is a tradition—and a big deal—I always had Thanksgiving dinner at the Posada household, and my parents would hang out with friends, so for us, our family celebration would always take place the next morning. I know it's different, but I never said we were like other families. This is living with the Carrs at its finest.

"May I bring a friend to our breakfast?"

"Lena and her husband are always welcome," she says in her typical mom's voice. "But please, don't bring that idiotic brother of hers. Your father would hit him and that would mess with our festivities."

"I was thinking about asking Martin to come." Think of something fast, Destinee, think of an excuse. Hurry, girl. "He lives close to me, and…"

I swear I hear her and my aunt squealing like crazy teenagers. "Mom, am I on speaker?"

"Your aunt wanted to hear your sweet voice."

Of course. It's more like she wanted the scoop, and my mother isn't in the mood to tell the whole story.

"That boy is a looker…" she says and at the same time my aunt adds something like 'so hot.' "I never understood why you chose the bad one… I think Desirae is crushing on him. Just tell him to keep his hands to himself."

Well, that would be harder than you think, Mom.

The smile on my face almost splits it in two. My family will be more supportive than I thought.

"Oh, baby. We're just about to leave the restaurant. Your aunt wants to take us to some stores she discovered last week." My poor father, he's about to endure the let's-empty-the-entire-mall adventure. The holidays are almost here, and my mother goes crazy around Christmas.

"See you in a couple of weeks," I say.

"See you then. Be good, baby."

"I always am."

That's my mom's standard farewell. Even if I were planning to be mischievous, I'd say the same.

"Hey," a voice says at my back, giving me a good scare. "I've been looking for you."

"What do you want, David?" My armor is on. I got this. I'm sure he'll get tired after another rejection. For him, I've never been worth the fight.

Honestly, I don't know how our toxic relationship lasted so long, it's beyond me.

"To talk to you," he says almost indignantly. "Can we go to your new place now?"

My questioning stare is on him. This time trying to figure out what I liked about this guy. He's one of the hottest men I've ever seen. Almost black hair, deep brown eyes, and a body to die for. But that isn't enough anymore. I want more. I want a man, not a prick.

"No, we can't." I walk forward, trying to go back to the safety of the house.

"Why are you being this bitchy?"

I stop in my tracks to look at him. This guy... "Because you deserve it."

My hands are shaking but I'm not budging. David is in the past. I want to move on for real this time.

"Destinee, baby, you love me," he has the gall to voice this as a fact. "In a couple of weeks, you will be begging me to take you back. You hate spending Christmas alone, and I bought your present already."

Maybe his words are somewhat true. But this time I'm making a real effort to overcome all this shit. Maybe I will be alone for Christmas. Maybe I won't fuck anyone by New Year, but better alone than in bad company. And David Posada is the worst company there is.

"I hope you saved the receipt. You'll need to return whatever shit you bought."

David opens his eyes in shock. "You aren't behaving like the sweet girl I fell in love with."

A sad smile pulls at my lips. "Be honest, David. At least with yourself. You never loved me, and I've never been a sweet girl."

"You've changed, Dee."

Finally, he's hitting the mark. "It's called growing up, David. I'm behaving like the adult I am, you should try to do the same."

I start walking toward the house without looking back. Then I notice Martin on the porch leaning on one of the wooden posts, his dark gaze on me.

"Did you see that?"

"Yes," he replies while standing. "Are you ok?"

"I will be. If you were here the entire time why didn't you try to intervene?"

"You managed it just fine by yourself, Dee. I'm proud of you."

His kind words warm my insides. This man is too much.

"Don't you want to fight my battles?" I ask him.

"No," he gives me his answer instantly. "I'll always be beside you, but we all have our own demons to fight. I was here, and I'll always be. But that one was your personal battle to win."

I need to be careful. Falling for Martin would be really easy and I'm not at the point where I'm ready for that again.

"You said we were going to take it slow," I remind him.

"And that's one of the reasons I stood back."

We walk together toward the door, and I look back. David's eyes are staring daggers at us and I swear he mouths something like, "Wait and see."

Fucker.

※※※

"Tell me, what's happening with my brother?" my best friend sighs while she, Erin, and I walk to her house. She's eager to show us the soon-to-be nursery.

"Nothing is happening, we broke up. For real this time."

140

She looks at me and rolls her brown eyes. Erin just smiles.

"I hope so," she states. "I've seen enough of you two. I love my brother dearly, but you aren't good for each other."

Our relationship in a nutshell. We definitely weren't good together.

"I must say… I almost fainted this morning at the sight of Martin and you together. A sight to behold, you were wearing similar outfits. So in tune."

"You're crazier than I thought," I reply. "It was just a coincidence. We aren't coordinating or anything."

"In a fantasy world, you two would be my favorite couple. Hands down. But I know nothing is happening there. For Martin, you're like a little sister."

Well, he did things to me that were far from brotherly.

"Mm-hmm…" It's the only thing I manage to mutter.

"You won't be the girl who jumps from one Posada brother to another. That's not who you are."

Hearing her words makes me cringe. I know there is no malice in them, just a reality check.

"You're gorgeous and men find you attractive," she continues with her rambling. "I'm sure in no time a good guy will lay the world at your feet. Perhaps it'll be a hot doctor." Then she gasps. "The perfect pair for you. A match made in heaven. A nurse practitioner and a doctor."

Then Erin speaks, changing the subject. This girl is a godsend. "I told Gabriel I want to hyphenate my last name after the wedding."

Elena gasps. "What did my brother say?"

"Not much," Erin replies with a besotted smile. "He knows my family is full of girls and the world is changing. In the end he even suggested the name Nicolas if we have a boy in the future."

Erin's last name is Nichols, so Nicolas would be amazing for a little boy.

"Nicolas Posada," Lena says dreamily. "The name has a good ring to it."

"Are you planning to send a letter to the stork right away?" I ask Erin.

She smiles and looks to Elena's garden, that's just a few yards away.

"No," she answers. "Gabriel and I want to travel and spend time together, just the two of us."

"You're living together now," Elena interjects.

"I know, but we both agree on this. There's no hurry. Plus, your little one will have its time before more cousins join the family."

A family, something I always wanted with David. Until my little fantasy infused bubble burst.

And I lost everything. Well, as much as you could lose something you never had, for starters.

Maybe Elena is right, maybe I need some time alone like I planned when moving to Silicon Valley. Martin is a great guy, but what do I have to offer at the moment?

A broken heart? A girl who doesn't believe in herself?

Being the reason to break up his family?

This isn't the first time I've been to Elena's new home. But I always find the place amazing, it's like she replicated a magazine spread. Everything is in the right place to make it look inviting and cozy. She guides us to a small room just a door away from her master suite.

"It's pretty empty right now, but the crib will arrive next week and then Cardan will hang the curtains..."

While she keeps gushing about her future baby's room, my head is still spinning. I need to talk with Martin, and I know for a fact he won't like what I have to say. But listening to Lena was a glimpse of what life is about. I told David I've changed, but also, I think I'm like a dragonfly that isn't ready to leave its cocoon yet. I'm still a pupa. My wings aren't big—or strong—enough to fly yet.

By the time I return to the Posadas' home, my mind is made up. Martin's worried eyes follow me like a hawk. He knows we need to talk, privately.

The drive back is a silent one. I know he's worried and I'm not trying to keep him in the dark on purpose. I've always been honest about everything. Starting with my feelings. I wasted eleven years trying to make everything perfect. I can't do that anymore.

"Martin?"

"Everything all right, *cariño?*"

"I hope—"

"Want to have dinner before going home?" Home, he's talking about his fabulous apartment. I can't go back there, though, knowing that I'm about to end us. An empty home is waiting for me… not as enticing, I know, but that's the place I need to be.

"Martin, I'm going back home." It's timid, but it's a start anyway.

"Ok…"

"I mean my own home," I say, taking a big breath. "I need time."

"Ok, whatever you need," he replies without a shadow of hesitation in his voice.

"Martin, what I mean is, I want time. Alone time."

His hands on the wheel open and close, as if he were gathering strength… or serenity, to finish this conversation.

"Look, you're a great guy…"

"Why do you make it sound like it isn't a good thing?"

With a sigh, I reply, "It is. You're amazing, Martin. That's the reason you deserve a whole woman. Not just scattered pieces of one."

He gives me a piercing glance, then his attention returns to the freeway in front of us. "You're more than that, Dee."

"At this moment, I'm not sure about who I am. That's the reason I want to spend some time by myself, Martin."

"I don't like the sound of this," he complains. I'm hurting him, I know, but better now than in the future. Love without healing would only drive us to a toxic relationship. That's not fair, for either of us.

"I want a future with you." That's the truth, but first I need time to heal. My mental health is my top priority at the moment. "I'd understand if you want to move on and live your life for a while…"

"I told you before…" The words leave his mouth like a growl. The interior of the car is dark now, but I can see his face slightly by the illumination of the cars around us. I know I'll regret driving this man away… he's so handsome. So caring. So everything a girl could dream of. "If you want me to wait for you, then I will."

"It's that easy?"

"Yes," he replies with another look. "That easy."

Martin takes me to my little pool house, and after unloading my laundry from the trunk of his car, he waits for me to open the door and checks that everything is fine. Before he says goodbye, my face is between his strong hands.

And his mouth descends over mine. This kiss tastes like desperation, he doesn't want to say goodbye, however, he's giving me what I asked for.

And it feels horrible.

# CHAPTER FOURTEEN

*Martin*

"Chloe!" I call out for my assistant. What's been happening around the office today? Not just today, but the entire week. Everyone seems to be working slower than ever. We just came back to work after Thanksgiving break, it seems they all need more time to recover.

I went to the orchard to have dinner with the family, just for the one evening. The next morning, even before the football game started, I was on my way back to Silicon Valley. Since then, I've been working nonstop with my team developing the dating app the girl from San Diego hired us for. This is the reason I hate being just a contractor. We don't have creative freedom, and Aiko, the app owner, is being really hard to please.

Aiko developed an algorithm that's protected under three patents. The thing works by taking all the user's social media posts as a data source. In my opinion, it works better than a long set of questions, and people tend to be more honest on said platforms. I understand the concept perfectly, but the creative process becomes a nightmare when the client is so adamant about her ideas for the interface. Even if it isn't that user friendly.

What do you want to do with an app that's not attractive for the user? Nothing, the thing will tank in a second. And I'm not ready to burn my reputation for a stubborn girl.

"Where the fuck is my report?"

Fuck, my patience is like a short wick these days. I'm a wagon full of TNT ready to explode.

"Chloe, dammit!" I call out to her again. "Where are my financial reports?"

She comes running at an insane speed. "Mr. Posada, they emailed them to you half an hour ago."

"Oh." It's the only thing that leaves my mouth. I'm about to add a string of words when my brother comes through my office door.

"Off with your staff's heads, *hermano?*" I'm sure he heard my moody outburst. Gabriel is on my short list for full access. Him, Ruben, and my father, can come and go as they please.

"Is there a particular reason for you to come by my office so early or are you just in the mood to be a nuisance?" I bark.

"Chloe, could you please bring me a coffee?" Gabriel requests.

"On the way, Mr. Posada," she smiles at him.

"Thank you," replies my brother, coming further into my office and undoing the button of his impeccably pressed suit as he sits in one of the leather chairs in front of my desk.

"What do you want?"

"What?" While crossing his leg with his ankle resting on his knee. "I'm not allowed to visit my little brother's office just because?"

Hoping he gets the clue, my stare remains glued on the screen. The code in front of me has some flaws, but it has potential. My team is doing fairly well, but they need to up their game or this will take us forever.

"I'm busy. Go and nag Ruben, or David."

"I'm not venturing to Berkeley at this time of day," he replies. David works over there for a big construction company. "And Ruben is on a business trip in New York. So you were the only sibling available for a visit."

"Well, I'm busy." Click, click, click. Copy, paste, delete. What the fuck is this line doing here?

See, brother? My hands are full here.

"What have you been up to these days?" he says in that mellow voice that grinds my nerves, like nails on a chalkboard. "I mean, aside from scaring your staff."

"Oh, you know, a little of this and a little of that."
What does he think, that I earn my money just sitting on my
ass?

"You're just acting like a dickhead because Dee kicked
your ass to the curb."

"She didn't kick my ass to the curb. She just asked me
for some time to think."

Finally the report downloads to my drive, this is an
urgent matter that needs action. I need to review this report
so I don't show up unprepared when I meet with a potential
investor that I've worked with before. Therefore, I can't
understand why Aiko doesn't give us creative freedom to
make her dating app shine. Our sales are skyrocketing, our
apps always go viral in no time.

This is what we do for a living. And believe me, my
work is stellar.

"Yesterday, she and Erin went for drinks," my brother
says. Those words capture my attention in a blink.

"What did she say?"

"Ah… so you are listening," my brother says with a
smirk, as if I have all the time in the world. Well, I do want all
the information about Destinee he's willing to provide.

These days without her haven't been easy. But I made
a promise to my girl to do whatever she needs. I'm not
starting a relationship with her by not honoring my word.

"Are you gonna tell me or what?"

Gabriel chuckles before replying, "She's doing fine. Apparently there is a sunrise yoga class on her landlord's lawn. She started last week. Erin says she looks good, happier."

A part of me is filled with joy knowing she's finding what she was looking for. The other part, the asshole who lives in the darkness, wants to scream at her and demand to know how she can be happy without me while I'm this miserable, living with the ghost of her wandering around my thoughts. My home. And my bed.

"Good to hear." I mumble, even if the hole in my chest grows larger.

"Really?" My brother questions. "Are you really happy about it?"

I look at him for a moment, considering my words while fire burns in my throat like lava.

My assistant chooses that moment to come in with Gabriel's coffee. A cup of dark roast with one sugar and no cream.

"What do you want me to say, Gabriel?" I ask him, after Chloe closes the door behind her. "Yes, this is killing me. Knowing she's out there, alone. Fighting her battles. I promised her the world, but how can I honor my promise and at the same time stay away from her?"

My brother's face morphs, the smirk vanishes while concern fills his eyes.

"Loving someone isn't an easy task. A successful relationship isn't for the faint of heart."

Hmm, easy for him to say, Erin is a great girl, and she looks content all the time.

"You make it look easy."

"Well, it isn't," he states. "Erin and I are different. She has her own ideas and isn't timid to fight for them. I struggle a lot with the need to protect her and let her shine at the same time. When she complains about her business issues, I want her to shut the damn thing down and for her to just stay at home. I mean, why not? I can provide for her easily."

As Oscar Wilde said, "Women are made to be loved, not to be understood."

"Why the fuck are they this complicated?" It frustrates me to be away from her. Where I can't shower her with my love, my devotion.

"Great achievement is usually born of great sacrifice, someone once said," Gabriel adds.

I had enough, this conversation needs to get straight to the point.

"What else did she say?" I'm craving answers, for more information. "Has David been around?"

"No," my brother assures me, that gives my soul a bit of peace. "She's spending her days at work, doing yoga, and hanging out with her new coworkers. Seems like she's decorating for Christmas and helping Erin with wedding stuff."

That makes me smile, imagining her on a yoga mat at sunrise stretching the lines of her beautiful body. One day I hope she'll get to exercise on my terrace, with the sun on her face and a smile on her lips. A smile I put on that rosy mouth.

"Is there more?"

"Yes. Lena is coming next week to do some shopping. She's been calling you, but you're too busy with your head in your ass to pick up the phone."

I didn't want to have to give excuses or hear whatever my sister had to say. I've been sending her calls straight to voicemail. Elena almost threw a tantrum when I informed her I was going back to the city the day after Thanksgiving. It was for the best, David and I could barely look each other in the eye, and my father knew something was happening between the two of us. With his health on the line, I didn't want to add more stress to the mix.

"She's coming, so is she staying at my home or yours?"

"In a hotel, actually," he informs me. "She and Cardan want to spend some time alone."

"And that matters to me because…"

"Because Elena wants to have dinner with all of us, including Destinee. And you're invited, dumbass."

Destinee was invited to our Thanksgiving celebration, like every year in the past. Sadly, she never showed up. A pang of pain stings my chest. "I don't know if she wants to see me. She hasn't sent me a single text."

"Have you?" The question throws me off-balance for a moment.

"Fuck, no." My words are hard. I'm on the defensive. "She asked me for time, I'm granting her wishes."

"You're dumber than I thought." Gabriel rolls his eyes. "You can send her a text just to say you're thinking of her. Wishing her the best, whatever."

"I'm not going to annoy her."

"Didn't you hear a word I just said?" My brother looks exasperated. "I said a text, not a novel-length email."

Hmm… maybe I've been reading this situation all wrong.

"Tread the waters carefully, then tell her you're looking forward to seeing her at the dinner. Leave the ball in her court, jackass."

I can do what he suggested. My brother's unannounced visit wasn't that bad, after all.

"And for fuck's sake, come to the restaurant with a clean, fresh shirt. And get a haircut."

I look at my outfit, there is nothing wrong with it. My long-sleeved shirt is a bit wrinkled, and my jeans are distressed; there's no dress code at my company. It's not like I've never worn worse.

"Are you sure Dee is going?"

"Positive," he assures me.

"Then I'll be there."

"Well, *hermano*. My work is done here, see you next week."

I'm too preoccupied with my own thoughts to pay attention to my brother leaving. I have a text to send and some shit to figure out.

Operation-win-my-girl-over has begun.

# CHAPTER FIFTEEN

## *Destinee*

**Martin:** *I'm busy every day... Busy thinking of you.*
*My work has just become a way to kill time.*

When Martin's name blinks on my screen my heart starts to beat faster. The last weeks have been hard—but beyond productive. I've spent my time working on myself. Talking with my new therapist, developing techniques to improve my self-esteem and how to notice toxic traits in any relationship. Not just in a romantic relationship. But the way to build healthy bonds with the people around me. My coworkers, my neighbors, the list is endless.

I contacted Crystal online. I was prolonging the time until our first meeting, for a lot of reasons. It was hard, not just telling her about the mistakes I made, but listening to what she had to say, especially about my past relationship with David. How David manipulated me by not taking no for an answer. When he had a tantrum on the flip of a switch. The gaslighting, how he always made me second guess myself. And the most important, the love bombing. Every time he said he loved me, it had a purpose. Never because he really felt it. All-in-all, realizing he was a textbook narcissist.

Fuck, why was I so blind?

Now, my heart is beating faster and my hands are shaking. A new patient is scheduled to come in a few minutes, I need to get my shit together before she arrives. What should I do? Should I reply to Martin's message? And what should I say? I'm thinking about you too, but give me time.

The phone on my desk rings, my patient is on her way. I decide to do nothing, I don't think Martin is waiting an answer.

A woman in her sixties comes in, her clinical history has been downloaded to the iPad in my hands. Her issue? Her and her husband had stopped having sex because it became too painful for her to bear.

I want to stand and give her a hug. The huge majority of women don't seek help because they're too ashamed to admit to this. Her blue eyes are filled with tears while she tells me the whole story.

"My husband is wonderful," she says while I hand her a box of tissues. "And our relationship has remained strong even if he can't stick his thing in, you know?"

With a flushed face, she tells me about the other ways they found to keep the heat between the sheets. But, she also tells me about the strain that's evident from the lack of intimacy. At first, her husband believed it was something transitory, but their worries increased when her condition worsened. He was the catalyst for her to come to the clinic today.

"It's been good, but I miss the feeling of him." Another wave of pink colors her cheeks. "He says he's happy. But I don't know…"

"You got a keeper," I reply.

"I do," she says with a little smile. "I'm a lucky woman."

"Now let's see if there is something I can do to get you even luckier." I give her a wink while guiding her to the exam table.

"This will be uncomfortable," I instruct her, taking the needed supplies from a shelf. "I'll be extra careful with you. Try to relax."

She says nothing, but her face mirrors her thoughts. Easier said than done. I really understand, but it's necessary. A visit here is never easy for a woman, but my mission is to provide my patients a safe environment for them to share their issues with me, and to look for a way to make it better for them.

Ten minutes later, my initial diagnosis is made. All the symptoms are there.

"Karyn," I call her by her first name, as she asked me to. "I want you to make an appointment with an urogynecologist. Luckily, we have one available here in the clinic. Dr. Wells is an amazing professional with tons of experience. Let me check her schedule."

"Is it that bad?" Her face is full of worry.

"Here comes the good news," I chirp. "I think you're suffering from a postmenopausal condition called vaginal atrophy. There is no need to worry, your condition could be easily fixed with reconstructive surgery."

"Really?" Her face lightens immediately.

"You're not alone, Karyn. As estrogen takes a nosedive, nearly half of postmenopausal women experience symptoms of some kind. Hormonal changes mess with our bodies big time. I'm proud of you for being this brave and coming to see me today."

Karyn deserves the praise. A lot of women's conditions just get worse because we aren't ready to share and just accept we're aging. There is no shame in it, time is inevitable for all of us.

"If you want, Dr. Wells has spots available for next week. Meanwhile I'll order a couple of tests just to confirm the diagnosis, ok?"

When I give her a hand to help her to stand from the table, her fingers on mine tighten. "You're a wonder. Thank you, Destinee."

"It's a pleasure," I give her hand a little squeeze before turning to give her privacy to get dressed. This is why I love my job so much. Helping women to get healthy again while dealing with compassionate and understanding professionals.

The rest of the morning goes by fast, I haven't had a single minute to spare until lunch time.

"Monica, I'm walking to the deli around the corner," I call out to my assistant. "Want something?"

"I'm good, thanks," she replies, adding something about eating healthy after Thanksgiving. "I want to fit into the sparkly dress I bought to wear on New Year's Eve."

"I'll be back in one hour," I say while taking my coat from the hanger.

The day is rainy and cold so I add my rainbow umbrella to the mix.

The deli is full of people and there's a long line to order, but I'm eyeing an empty stool at the counter against the windows.

There's a tall guy in front of me, but I just see his back. We're located in an area full of tech businesses and this man is wearing a plaid flannel shirt, jeans and work boots. Exuding total mountain man vibes. So freaking hot. I'm on a diet and men are off the menu, but there's no harm in looking.

In the mood for something warm and comforting, I order a sweet potato and chickpea buddha bowl.

"The guy standing in line before you paid for your order," the girl behind the counter says and I have to blink twice for my brain to understand.

"Pardon me?"

"Yes," she replies and points to the man who's standing at the side, waiting for his meal, no doubt.

"Thank you," I mouth and give him a smile. Then my attention is back on the cashier. "I'll pay for the next customer's meal."

This is the perfect time to give back.

I straighten my coat before walking to where the man is standing. He's really handsome, he has a straight nose, clean shaved jaw, and dirty blond hair.

"Hey," I greet him. "I guess a thank you is in order."

"It was my pleasure," he smiles back. "I'm Gavyn Masson."

I give him my hand. "I'm Destinee."

"A beautiful name for a beautiful girl," he replies. "Tell me, Destinee, you come here often?"

"I do." But I don't give him more information, the world is full of weirdos, and I don't need to add a stalker to my list.

His name is called, and after a minute mine is too. We walk together to a table in a corner and spend the next half hour talking about simple things. Like music and books.

"You have excellent taste in movies," he says with a smirk. "But a terrible one in music."

"Believer forever," I counter, talking about Justin Bieber fandom. "Don't you dare judge me!"

He just laughs then takes something from his wallet. A business card.

"I'd like to see you again," he tells me, looking into my eyes. "I own a construction company here in Redwood city, here is my contact information, including my cell phone."

I look at the card as if it burned my fingers.

"Here is when you offer your number back."

Instead of asking him for his phone for me to type my number on it, I take a pen from my pocket and then his hand. It's slightly rough but his nails are short and clean. To his surprise, I start writing on his palm.

As soon as I finish my task, I stand and start walking toward the exit. With a final glance over my shoulder, I say, "See you soon."

"I guarantee you will," I hear him say.

The time is here. My bestie is in town and we're having dinner in an upscale restaurant in San Francisco. Too tired to drive, I call an Uber.

**Gavyn:** When are you having dinner with me?

Since our first encounter at the deli, Gavyn and I have been texting back and forth. When I arrived back at the clinic that day, a message was waiting for me already.

Gavyn is nice, charming, and I like his wit. Also, he hasn't sent a dick pic or asked me for a picture of my naked tits. But he's not Martin. He doesn't give me butterflies every time my phone chimes with a notification.

I've been working hard on moving forward. I've finally deleted all my pictures of David, as well his old texts, and emails. Even his number isn't in my contacts list anymore. My therapist said it was a step in the right direction. I'm cutting ties with the hurtful part of my past and learning new coping strategies to deal with it.

Tonight will be challenging. I know David will be there, but Elena wants us all together. Honestly, I'm more anxious—and excited—to see Martin. He has been sending messages every now and then, just to tell me he's thinking of me. Nothing too pushy, but appreciated all the same.

I'm learning to be just Destinee, and I'm happy with the woman I'm discovering behind the layers of insecurities and self-doubts. I guess they'll always be there, the trick is to deal with my ghosts and keep them at bay.

The car stops in front of the restaurant and before opening the door, I check my outfit one last time. I'm dressed to impress—for myself—mostly. But the girl inside me screams she wants Martin to like the way she looks. I'm wearing black from head to toe. A cashmere fitted sweater and high-waisted vegan leather pants. My feet are clad in my studded high-heels and a coat is hanging from my arm. My red lipstick is on point, this girl is ready for anything.

After telling the hostess Cardan's name she tells me my friends are waiting already. My heart is pounding against my rib cage. But it slows down a bit when I notice just Elena, Cardan, Erin, and Gabriel are there sipping wine and chatting.

The table is set for six. My stomach drops at the count of the chairs. Isn't he coming? I have very little time to think about it because Lena jumps up from her seat to hug me. Once the round of greetings is complete, I take the spot beside my bestie. Cardan is sitting at the head of the table, and Gabriel and Erin, at the other side.

"You look stunning," Elena praises me. She's glowing, and the green maternity dress she's wearing enhances her best features. "Did you lose weight?"

"Maybe," I reply with a smile. "I have been taking yoga classes every morning before work."

"Lucky you," she says with disgust. "My doctor said I need to walk every day for at least half an hour. As if running around the orchard wasn't enough exercise." She ends her statement with an eye roll.

"I like Pilates," Erin joins in on the conversation. "It helps me a lot with my endurance at work."

"Yeah, at work," Gabriel chuckles and Elena almost gags.

Erin gives her fiancé the stink eye and keeps talking. "Running, carrying floral arrangements around a ballroom is serious business."

"How is the shop doing?" I ask her.

Erin explains how her flower shop is doing. Since this is the low season for weddings, she is offering her clients a seasonal decoration service, and the thing is blooming. Literally.

"With all the wedding expenses, I'm just happy to earn some extra—"

"Babe," Gabriel's voice cuts her off. "I told you I'm more than happy to pay for everything, if you weren't so stubborn and…"

They exchange an adoring look and I almost melt into a puddle.

"I know, but…"

"Good evening," a deep voice says from above our heads.

I didn't see him approaching.

And he looks gorgeous. Like panty-melting gorgeous.

# CHAPTER SIXTEEN

*Martin*

Just my luck. Today, I intended to arrive before her, cool, calm and collected, but my meeting with a previous investor I'm trying to buy out of my company was extended because he's playing hard to get. Hence, I'm running five fucking minutes late.

Believe me. I hate arriving late. If you're ten minutes early, you're on time. If you're on time, you're late. And if you're late, there's no point in showing up. But there is no way in hell I'm missing dinner tonight.

A few days ago, I started to message her. Just with simple reminders, a reminder of how much she means to me, and how she's still constantly on my mind. Some messages are a bit corny, others a little flirty, making attempts to put a smile on her face.

Arriving at the hostess stand, I give the girl my brother-in-law's name and she smiles, playing with her red hair and looking at me under her lashes. I know what she's doing. *It isn't working, sweetheart, I'm taken.*

They're already sitting, one chair at the head of the table is empty, waiting for me. Next to the girl of my dreams, who is chatting with my siblings.

Her hair is curlier tonight, and her lips are stained in a perfect shade of red that I want to see smeared on my dick. My girl is simply breathtaking.

"Good evening," I say, calling their attention. Destinee's eyes are on me in a second, she scans me from head to toe. She's free to look as much as she wants. This morning I decided to wear one of my best suits, ready to give off the best impression. Seeing the way Destinee's blue gaze turns darker, I'd say mission accomplished.

"You look gorgeous," I whisper into Dee's ear, low enough for only her to hear. She gives me a small smile but says nothing. The waiter fills my glass with red wine while my brother asks me about my work. He knows what I'm trying to do. At the moment, my bank account is big enough to take over my company. Investors aren't required anymore and I like the sense of control over the entire operation. Every now and then, I would make temporary deals with people I trust, but nothing beyond that.

Erin, Elena, and Destinee keep talking about the wedding and the upcoming Christmas season, but my ears are attuned to hear anything that leaves Dee's red mouth.

When our meals arrive, the atmosphere around us becomes more intimate. My sister is busy talking with her husband, while Gabriel is whispering something to Erin. That gives me the perfect chance to capture my girl's attention.

Her body is turned toward me, the black sweater she's wearing gives me a little peek of her cleavage. A sight to behold.

"How are you doing?" she asks in a murmur.

"Good. Busy at work." My answer is short and clipped. To be honest, I don't know what else to say. That's pretty much a brief recount of my days.

"Do you—" she starts to say, but cuts herself before ending the sentence.

"What do you want to ask? If I'm missing you?"

She turns for a beat to see what the other couples are doing then a simple word leaves her mouth. "Yes."

"Then ask, Dee," I tell her. "I'm giving you what you asked for even if it's killing me. You said you wanted time…"

"I know…" she whispers, lowering her head to take another bite of the pasta in front of her.

I know she's only eating as a diversion but the food here is excellent.

"Tell me how you are doing these days. Trying new stuff?"

"Yes," she replies. This time her eyes are shining with excitement. "I joined a yoga at sunrise class in my

169

neighborhood, then I painted my home, and started decorating. I've been told *I was born with an enormous need for affection, and a terrible need to give it.* That's how I ended up in a toxic relationship for years. I've been working on how to manage that need inside me. I wanted to be loved, very loved, Martin. I… I'm…" she stops as if ashamed.

"Tell me," I implore her to continue.

"I'm seeing a therapist," she reveals, like sharing a secret. "You're the first person I've told about it. It hasn't been easy, but I'm learning and growing from it."

This time I don't give a fuck about who's watching. Over the table, my hand reaches for hers and gives it a little squeeze.

"I'm so fucking proud of you."

"You are?" Her eyes are misting but that spark is still there.

"Of course I am. You're fighting the hardest war. You're in a battle with your old self who refuses to let you go and be free. To be happy."

She rewards me with another smile, a big one this time. "I've missed you too."

I thank my lucky stars for that. "Me or my bed?" The memories we made that morning have been haunting me since the moment I had to go back to my apartment alone.

That makes her laugh hard. "And don't forget about your shower."

"Or my laundry room."

"True," she replies as the tension vanishes. We're back to the easy talk, the jokes, the way it has always been between the two of us.

"Are you making advances with the dating app?"

"It's driving me nuts," I answer honestly, but go more in depth at the sight of her worried face. "Not the app per se, but the girl who hired us. It'll be a very long time before I decide to work for other people again."

"Oh no," she says in a soft voice. "What happened?"

I give her the last day's play-by-play.

"Are you planning to go home for Christmas?"

"I haven't made plans yet." That's the truth. Even if I'll visit my father around the holidays. "Maybe I'll go somewhere, I'm not sure. My schedule is pretty open right now. Are you going home?"

She smiles. "My mother would disown me if I even dare miss Christmas at home."

Destinee's mother decorates her entire house and on Christmas Eve opens the place for people to visit and have a drink while looking around.

Even if the whole family isn't here or the fact we aren't at our home, we end up the same way. Talking out loud, laughing a lot, also eating a ton. After dessert, my brother, Cardan, and I argue over whose turn it is to pay the bill. In the end, I'm faster than them, giving the waiter my black credit card.

"Where is your car parked?" Elena asks Destinee as we leave the restaurant.

"I didn't drive, I'm calling an Uber to take me home." Her phone is in her hands, no doubt opening the rides app.

"The heck you will," I growl. Those words leave my mouth before I have the chance to stop them. "I mean, you can come with me. I'm driving south anyway."

"How convenient," I hear my brother snicker and I want to shut his mouth with my fist.

"It's settled," says Lena as if she orchestrated the whole thing. "That way I'll be able to go to bed without any worries."

"Babe, you pretty much are asleep before your pretty head touches the pillow," Cardan chuckles.

My sister gives him a death glare then turns her attention to us.

"I loved spending time with my favorite people." She beams before hugging Destinee. "Let's do this again soon, ok?"

"Sure thing," Destinee replies without any real commitment.

After another round of farewell hugs, we're on the sidewalk walking to my car that's parked a block over from the restaurant. That offers me the perfect chance to ogle the way those leather pants fit Dee's sweet ass. My gut screams for me to throw her over my shoulder and take her home where I can peel the damn things off her body and spend the rest of the time lost in those curves.

"Oh! We're driving guilt-free again," she says when we arrive at the place my electric car is parked.

"I left the gas-guzzler at home tonight." I open the passenger door for her, and make sure she's buckled before walking around to hop into my seat.

While driving, I open and close my mouth several times, racking my brain for something smart to say. I've never felt this way around a woman. I've had some relationships in the past. None of them were successful because my heart was busy pining over a girl I never thought I could have. Now here we are.

"Thanks for the ride," she says as soon as we arrive at her place.

I run to open the door for her again while figuring out what to say. Something engaging… romantic…

I take her hand, enjoying the feeling of her soft palm between mine. She smiles at me as she unlocks her front door, our time together is about to end. *Make your move, jackass.*

Now or never.

I move closer so our torsos are almost touching. My hand cups her cheek while the other tilts her head back. Holding her in place. I hear her suck in a breath, that makes me stop the descent of my head. But she wets her lips with that little tongue.

"I want you… so fucking much." Then our lips meet, as if they were destined just like my fate was sealed years ago by this girl. My mouth is pressed against hers softly at first and after she grants me entrance, my grip on her becomes tighter.

This kiss is melting my bones like hot lava. I deepen the kiss at a different angle, this girl is utter perfection. Everything about her entices me. The silky strands of her hair slipping through my fingers, the floral perfume she wears. Even the way her hands are tangled around my neck holding me close.

The touch of her tongue dancing with mine makes me a goner, a moan escapes from her mouth overwhelming all of my senses as we continue to kiss. I need her behind a closed door, right the fuck now.

"Martin, I'm not ready…"

I pull away and rest my forehead on hers. Both my hands falling off her neck as both of us breathe heavily.

"*Cariño*, I…"

"I need more time… I…" She trembles while saying, "There is still too much I need to deal with."

Something inside me breaks… again. Maybe this is a stupid dream. Maybe I should move on.

Maybe she's not the right girl for me.

"Go inside, Dee," I tell her. "I'll wait until you lock the door."

She does as she's told, and after hearing the noise of the deadlock catch, I turn away toward my car. Admitting defeat. That once I leave, I'm...

Outta here. Out of her life.

Forever.

# CHAPTER SEVENTEEN

*Destinee*

*Happy girls are the prettiest.*

I've copied the quote onto a post-it note and stuck it to the mirror over my dresser to remind me of the reason I'm doing all of this. Some days I wake up feeling hopeful and deliriously happy. Others, like today, the burden on my shoulders is so heavy for me to bear.

December passed in a blur. I went home for Christmas, then spent the next day at Elena's home watching movies and lingering on her couch while munching on cookies and leftovers.

"Some day, my friend, you will find the oil magnate you've been waiting for," she tried to cheer me up by joking about the type of man I wanted back when we were just kids.

I pondered for a moment before replying. "You know what? My priorities have changed. Now I just want a good man who really loves me."

Lena looks at me with her eyes full of wonder. "Dee, seems like you finally grew up."

I reply by throwing a pillow at her head. But it was true. I've grown up and learned.

She tells me about their dinner—a pang in my chest urges me to ask about him but I managed to remain quiet and listened to her babbling about the gift Cardan gave to her. A babymoon to the Bahamas. They were leaving the very next day.

For New Year's Eve, my coworkers threw a party, and as planned I went wearing my sparkliest dress and danced all night fueled by bubbly champagne.

Martin is always there, like a ghost wandering around in my mind—and heart—I've been incapable of exorcising him. I guess it's something else I have to learn to live with. Not that I've been stalking him on social media or anything. No, I just check his account a thousand times a day and die every time that smile appears in a picture wishing I was there with him and that I was the reason he smiled so broadly.

January has been busy at the clinic, our schedule is always fully booked. It's exciting, but it consumes a lot of my energy. It's almost six in the evening, and on Tuesdays I leave early to attend my therapy session with Crystal. It's an online meeting, I just hope I find some inner strength somewhere to endure it.

As I open my laptop and log in to the online portal, my chest begins to pound and mentally I hope that Crystal will ask easy questions today. The chances are microscopic, almost nonexistent. The woman is brutal. And goes straight for the jugular every time. Forcing me to face my issues before learning techniques to deal with them.

We start talking, the usual questions about my week and what's been bothering me lately.

"I kissed him," I confess, since the night at the restaurant, the memory of his mouth dancing over mine is still haunting me. "Or he kissed me. It was fantastic… and scary."

"Elaborate," she tells me.

"Well, I really liked the kiss… I was craving it since the moment he arrived at the restaurant."

It felt so right. His touch was perfection, my mouth tingles just at the memory. It hasn't faded. Martin set me on fire, using his body as fuel.

"Then, why did you feel scared about the kiss?"

I take a huge lungful of air, thinking hard, "It terrifies me how big his hold is over me. Martin could easily make me fall for him. And it terrifies me, Crystal. My relationship with David almost crushed me, breaking up with Martin would kill me."

"What would happen if you found a way to be together?"

There are no easy questions with this girl. Her mission is to make me think hard. About everything.

"What if he leaves me again," I blurt out. Almost puking out the words.

"When did he leave you, Destinee?"

I tell her the whole story about our childhood friendship and how it ended when he turned eighteen. And things got worse after David and I became a couple. Martin didn't even dare look at me. Whenever we were alone in a room, he fled.

"You don't trust him," she says in a firm voice. "The lack of trust is holding you back."

Hearing that shocks me, as I give it some thought it starts to make sense.

"Could be that…" I whisper, mostly to myself.

"Destinee, there are no guarantees in a relationship," she states. "If you decide to jump into one, you should be able to trust that person wholeheartedly. If and when you decide to take a leap, you have to forget what happened and just look forward."

More consideration on my part.

"He's also my ex-brother-in-law. Well, not technically, but close enough." Which is another reason to stay away. Posada men are dangerous for the female population. They can charm a nun if they set their minds on it.

"You can't blame him for that, Destinee."

Dang, that's a valid point. Martin didn't choose the family he was born into.

"Destinee, you must consider his reasons. His mother had a valid point, and she was also protecting you. What would you do if you had a preteen girl who spends a lot of time alone in a young man's company?"

"I would think it isn't appropriate," I reply in a low voice.

"And what would you do if you were in his shoes?"

If the man I love were in a relationship with one of my sisters, I'd probably stay far away from them. It'd be too painful to witness.

"Destinee, I'm not here to tell you what to do," she adds. "If you feel the need to step away from Martin and wait until you're able to rekindle your friendship, then go down that path. You need to think about it though, so this is your homework for the week. I'll see you next Tuesday"

We end the session and I feel even more exhausted than before. This isn't easy for me, but they say you need to work hard for everything that's worth it, right?

Later while lying on my bed, trying to sleep I read and re-read Martin's texts. Then take a look at our pictures, just a couple from our tech tour. My finger touches the screen craving his touch. But the cold glass is a reminder we aren't together.

And maybe it's for the better.

On Wednesday, I wake up with an idea.

I'm moving on.

Unplugging my phone from its charger, I send a message to Gavyn. He has been asking me out for weeks now. So maybe this is my chance, maybe life is sending me messages for me to keep going with my life and fish in a new pond.

Perhaps Gavyn isn't the right man for me. But going out with people, enjoying myself isn't prohibited. I'm a young woman and I'm not asking the man to marry me, just to have dinner, talk, and maybe go out dancing.

**Destinee:** Hey. Are you still up for going out?

He replies after a couple of minutes.

**Gavyn:** I'm free tonight if you are.

**Destinee:** What about Friday? I'd hate to go to work after a late night.

**Gavyn:** You're the boss, beautiful girl.
Saturday at seven?

I can't believe I'm actually doing this. I mean, I've gone out with other men through the years, but never with the real intention to move on, I did it just to make David jealous. This feels different, this *is* different.

**Destinee:** I'll text you my address.

**Gavyn:** It's a date.

It definitely is.

I decided to do some shopping during my lunch hour. I deserve a reward after being this brave, dating isn't for the faint of heart. I ended up buying a silky slip dress and an oversized leather jacket. My new pieces will look amazing with a pair of booties I already own. Feeling satisfied and animated for my date night, I go back to work.

When the time for Gavyn to pick me up arrives, I'm looking forward to our night out. I've spent a huge amount of time doing my hair, and my makeup is flawless. My legs look amazing with this dress and the booties. Yoga is working marvels for my body. I've got more energy, elasticity, and the lines of my muscles are more visible than ever.

"You look breathtaking," Gavyn greets me at my door, handing me a bouquet of sunflowers, a thoughtful touch to start the night.

"Thank you," I reply. "For the flowers too, they are beautiful."

"No more than you." Gavyn is behaving like the perfect gentleman. He has also dressed the part. Wearing dark jeans, with a blue button-down shirt and a sport coat.

"Where are we going?"

He smiles while we walk to his truck. "I made reservations for a seafood place I think you'll like."

When he opens the door, his blue eyes look into mine with a bit of panic shadowing them. "I forgot to ask you if you're allergic."

I laugh a little. "I love seafood. You made a good choice." I give him a wink and close the door.

Something is wrong with me. Really wrong.

I'm enjoying Gavyn's company. He's funny, smart, and attentive. He hasn't taken his phone out and his attention has been on me the whole night. But every time he touches me nothing happens. I'm sitting here waiting for the butterflies to start fluttering in my belly. For the spark to ignite. I smile and give him the right answers, witty remarks, and flirtatious looks.

Maybe this is like the love for oysters? Something you learn to love in time?

I don't want to stay in a shell, not even if there is a pearl waiting there.

I want the fireworks.

"And I've been working on my own since then," he ends his story about how awful it was for him to work for a company in the area after being honorably discharged from the Army.

"Now you're dealing with employees, and taxes, and picky clients…"

"I love my work," he remarks. "I do my very best every day. If I have to deal with some nuisances, it's ok with me."

"Because it's worth it."

"Damn right," he says before drinking his white wine. "I'd go nuts working from nine to five in an office. My job suits me and makes me happy."

"It's all about small sacrifices."

"Sometimes they're not so little," Gavyn tells me with a nod. "Some days are frustrating. Some days I'm worried about money or suppliers raising their prices, the list is endless. But life is about taking risks, Dee. A life in a crystal bubble can be beautiful, but there is nothing satisfying in that."

His words hit me hard. Gavyn, without realizing it is giving me the advice I've been looking for.

"If you want something, take a leap," he continues talking. "Surviving is for cowards. Living to the fullest, that is where true bravery is shown."

Be brave. Living to the fullest.

Suddenly, I know exactly what I want to do.

"Gavyn," I say. "I'm having the best time here with you—"

"Why does that sound like a bad thing?" He cuts me off.

"No, no," I tell him, moving my head. "The thing is…"

I tell him the whole story, and to his credit, he listens to me patiently.

"I can't let you pay. It's too much," I start fussing when the waiter brings the check. "This wasn't a date."

He gives me a wink and replies, "Maybe, but I'm still a gentleman." One day this man will find the right girl. However, that girl won't be me.

He drives me home, we say goodbye with a quick hug along with the empty promise to stay in touch. As soon as his truck is out of my driveway, I jump into my car with one destination in mind.

I'm a woman on a mission.

# CHAPTER EIGHTEEN

## *Martin*

There is someone knocking on my door on a Friday night.

Gabriel told me he's helping Erin with some arrangements she's required to deliver tonight. Ruben is busy chasing skirts. And David, well, we aren't on the best of terms.

I have no neighbors; I own the entire floor and the apartment below mine is under renovations.

The pounding becomes desperate. Who the fuck is here? I look at the camera on my cell phone and I swear the air vanishes from the entire apartment.

It can't be.

It can't be her.

What is Destinee Carr doing at my door at this late hour? What's she doing here *at all?*

"Martin, I know you're in there," she calls out loud.

If I'm being honest, I don't know what to do. This girl brought me to my knees so many times, am I ready to surrender again? Fuck, yes!

I stand from my spot on the couch and walk to the door with shaky legs.

"What are you doing here?" I ask as soon she comes within view. She looks more gorgeous than ever. I manage to stay standing even if my knees are ready to collapse and worship my goddess. She's wearing a sexy dress with… those legs. I want to have them around my hips. Or head while I enjoy my dessert.

"Your tech tour wasn't complete," she says breathlessly. "You never took me to your office."

My brain is clouded by a fog of joy and confusion.

"I'm not going to my office now, Destinee."

What does she want?

"We can go in the morning," she says with a small shy smile.

"What does that even mean?"

"I want to stay here with you, Martin."

My heart stops. "For how long?" I ask with a dry mouth.

"Forever if you want me," she replies. But all I can hear in my head is her asking, If I want her?

*Want her?*

I can't help myself, leaning over her, I throw Destinee over my shoulder, marching into my home with determined steps. I swear she breathes something like *yeah*. But first I set her over my kitchen counter.

A mix of confusion and lust appears in her beautiful eyes.

Turning, I open my refrigerator and take out a beer.

"Can I offer you something?"

She blinks a couple of times as if I spoke in an unknown language. "I thought you…"

I lean into the stainless steel of the appliance and give her a smirk. "What, that I threw you over my shoulder to toss you onto my bed?"

"Well…" she whispers. "Yes."

After twisting the cap, I take a long gulp of my beer.

"I will," I inform her. "All in good time."

She bites her lower lip, trying to hide a smile. I want to be the one tugging that lip with my teeth.

"Do I need to wait long?"

"That depends," I reply with another smirk. My heart is pounding hard, the girl I've craved all my life is in front of me… but something is holding me back. We need to talk before taking any step forward.

"On…"

"Why are you here tonight, Destinee?"

"I miss you, Martin," she says, and my blood pressure spikes.

"If you're playing a twisted game with me, stop now." My voice is hard. "You said you missed me, then when things got serious you said you needed more time and ran."

"I'm done running."

"What does that mean for us?"

"I've been doing a lot of reflection," she starts. "The other day I told my therapist everything about us. She thinks my lack of trust is holding me back. She thinks I'm afraid to open myself up to you."

That hits me in the middle of the chest like a wrecking ball.

"Martin, now I can understand your reasons, before when we were younger I just felt like you abandoned me. You were the only one who understood me… and then one day you ghosted me."

My beer is forgotten. I take two steps closer and place my hands on her knees.

"I'm sorry, Dee." I apologize with deep sincerity.

"I know," she replies, her hands fly up to my neck and she begins to play with the short strands of my hair, just over the fabric of the hoodie I'm wearing. "I want to live life to the fullest, Martin. And I want you to be right next to me."

"As your partner in crime?" I ask. Destinee is bulldozing my defenses.

"As my partner in everything."

I part her legs. Our torsos are a breath apart. I'm ready to pull her in and kiss her. I'm ready to give in and never let her go. I'm ready to make her mine.

"I want that too, *cariño*. With you, I want everything." My hands are now around her neck, placing her where I want.

"It's yours," she says while I lean in to touch her lips with mine.

Her skin feels warm under my cold fingers. Her eyes are like pools, like an abyss that I want to drown in. Her breath stutters at my touch. Pride spreads through my chest knowing that I'm the cause. My kitchen is silent, but I swear her heartbeat could be heard pounding like a drum in the same rhythm as mine.

The hands on my neck pull me in deeper. "Kiss me harder, Martin. Make me yours"

"Are you trying to give me orders?"

"Isn't the gentlemanly thing to say, your wish is my command?"

"Oh yeah?" I give her a smile while my thumb traces the line of her mouth. I feel the last of my resistance falling away.

My lips find hers as her soft moan can be heard in the silence. And while my tongue searches hers out, my body reacts. I'm ready to make my claim. No more words are needed tonight. I'm sure our bodies will speak for us.

Her legs wrap around me while she grinds her warm center against my growing erection. I'm starving for the taste of her—everywhere.

My tongue follows the line of her jaw, traveling to her slender neck. Feeling her pulse speeding under my caress.

"You know…" she murmurs. "I was on a date tonight."

What? I stop in my tracks. "You were?"

"Yes. And all I could think about was the way you make my body come alive. This feeling, the spark…"

My hands descend down her body until they are under the hem of her short dress.

"Did you let him touch you this way?"

"No," she replies breathily.

"Did you wear this for him?"

The caveman living inside me roars. Jealousy pumping hard through my veins.

She's mine.

"I wore it for me." Her voice is soft but sure.

I want her—now. But she deserves more than a quick fuck on my kitchen counter. I need her on my bed, where I can spend the entire night worshiping her body without restrictions.

With my hands under her ass, I lift her. Immediately she holds onto me, her limbs like vines around my waist.

Feeling her skin under my fingertips overwhelms me. She feels so perfect. I need to taste her, more than that. I need to feast on her.

"Let's get you out of this dress," I growl. I hate the fact she dressed to the nines to go out on a date. I don't know the man's name and I hate him already. She's mine, only mine.

As soon as the black fabric leaves her body exposing her milky skin, which is barely covered by lacy lingerie, my mouth goes dry at the sight of the most perfect pair of tits I've ever seen.

I'm so hard it's painful. I can't wait to get lost in her. Dropping kisses along the edges of her lingerie, I drag her bra straps down her arm, slowly removing it, exposing those pert little nipples I've dreamt of on so many lonely nights, they're begging for my attention. I bite those hard points, being rewarded by more moans. I continue to remove her sexy panties off her body.

Destinee Carr is naked and beneath me. Finally, I part her legs, and I'm rewarded with the unobstructed view of her. Fuck. I almost come in my pants.

I slide my palms down her thighs, spreading them wider. "You are soaking wet for me." She cries out when my finger traces her slit, taking the time to spread her juices around her bundle of nerves.

"Martin," she moans again. Is she pleading or demanding? To be honest, I don't even care.

Instead of answering her with words, I use my mouth to trail kisses down her body until I'm gifted with the sight of her glorious cunt. She's the appetizer, the entrée, and the dessert all rolled into one, a meal worthy of devouring. She's more delectable than I've ever imagined, and sweeter than in my dreams. The taste of her honey on my tongue is purely addictive, I don't want to ever stop. But I can't wait to feel her walls clenching around my cock. Her fingers are in my hair pulling it hard, while her hips move seeking for more. Destinee is so responsive and I love it. Everything about her draws me in.

"You're killing me," she says, gasping for air, when two of my fingers delve inside her.

I set a pace, observing her reactions while the sounds she makes get louder, to the point where her body goes rigid and her back arches. I keep working on her sweet pussy until she goes limp and her legs close around my shoulders. I want to beat my chest like a caveman knowing that I've brought her to the peak.

"Now I want you inside me," she says.

"Who am I to say no to you?" In two seconds flat I'm naked and looking for protection in my bedside table.

"No," she stops me with her hand around my hard cock. "I'm safe, I promise. I want to feel you."

I'd never do anything to harm her. *Ever.* "Are you sure? You're safe with me, but if you want me to…"

She says nothing, just guides me to her opening, I thrust inside her hard.

"Do you feel this?" I grumble. "This is the only cock you'll feel for as long as we live."

We were made for each other. Her muscles grip me hard while I keep thrusting inside her. She feels so freaking good, I'm not going to last long.

"Fuck. I'm gonna come again," she moans.

"Do it. I want to feel your pussy squeeze me," I reply.

I can't think of anything else other than her. The way she moves, pushing against me. The way she smells, the taste of her on my tongue.

I lean down, kissing her skin, trailing a wet path to her mouth. She welcomes me eagerly as I pound harder into her. Her nails, digging into my flesh as her lips part for me. I pick up the pace, my desire is to chase the light at the end of the tunnel. And I want her right there when we reach the station. I change the angle and with a few well-placed thrusts…

"Martin," she breaks the kiss, crying out loud while her muscles tense around me.

I'm a goner. I crash into bliss with her.

My heart is pounding hard against my rib cage, so hard I'm sure she can feel it. With what little strength I have left, I drop to my back bringing her into my side. Unable to break our connection.

"You feel so good," I say, running my fingers up and down her back.

Dee pushes herself up onto my chest, her hands on my shoulders. Her gorgeous tits pushed together, awakening my arousal again. At this pace I'll be ready for round two in no time.

She smiles and starts to cant her hips, swaying back and forth softly. Her still wet pussy is gliding against my length. Even better, she's not only ready but looking for it.

"You know," she says while moving. "I didn't come here tonight with the intention to get fucked."

"No?" I ask, lifting my eyebrows.

"No," she shakes her head, making that blonde hair float in the air. "I came to claim you."

"Then do it," I reply, leaving her to take control as she guides me to her entrance.

Destinee is such a turn on. Her words, the way she acts as if she knows what I want and at the same time gets whatever she craves from me. She leans back, looking like a goddess, her tits bouncing with her movements, I reach for them, grazing my fingers over the hard points of her rosy nipples.

She keeps moving up and down until we are both close to coming. Taking her hands in one of mine and placing it at the small of her back, I use my free hand to grip her hips as I take control and start thrusting hard from beneath.

A loud cry leaves her body. Sweat coats her skin as her movements become faster and sharper, trying to match my rhythm.

"Dee…" I growl and pull her down, claiming her lips while my mouth swallows her moans of ecstasy. I let myself go as she spasms around me, milking every drop of my pleasure.

She falls onto my chest, panting for air. Relaxed and sated. I can't imagine being happier than I am right now.

Well, maybe I can. I want this every day. Every night. I want to scream to the entire world she's mine and make her happy forever. Maybe this isn't the fairy tale she envisioned when she was younger, but I can show her editing a story just makes it better.

❋❋❋

"Are you taking me to your office in the morning?" she asks me when finally we can catch our breath.

"Eager to leave my bed already?"

"Fuck, no," she replies and kisses my chest. My arm is around her shoulders holding her close. "I just want to stay here with you."

"In my bed?" I ask her. "In my home?"

"For more reasons than just your shower this time," she says. "I want to stay in your life, Martin. I was serious when I told you I'm ready to move forward."

"I want that too, *cariño*. More than you'll ever know."

"I think I do."

"You do?" I tease her, poking her in the ribs, making her squeal.

Her hands are in my hair, caressing softly. "Maybe we should move slow…" she starts to say. My body tenses. "But not to a stop." I can feel myself relax again.

"I'm not ready for your family to know yet."

I can understand that. An announcement would—and will be—a breaking point between my brother and I. My father will be caught between us.

"But you're coming to the wedding, right? I want you there."

"I'm going," she assures me. "My hotel reservation is already made, and my dress is hanging in my closet."

"I want you there as my plus one." More than that, I want her there as my girlfriend. The woman who I want by my side forever.

"That's a downgrade," she complains.

"Being there with me is a downgrade to you?" I fake an offended expression. The truth is I'm looking forward to seeing what comes out of her mouth.

"I'm teasing, mister," she says with a soft giggle. "Will you save me a dance?"

The feel of her breath along the skin of my neck makes my dick stir. I hope she's ready to go again.

"You can have all my dances. Then, I'll take you to our room, undress you slowly and start the real party."

"A party just for two."

I reply by taking her hands in mine, laying her on her back. My body looming over her curves. With my legs, I spread her thighs while my erection hits home.

"Martin," I hear her gasp.

And for a long time, just the sound of our moans fill the room.

# CHAPTER NINETEEN

*Destinee*

"These household rules suck," I complain while he tightens the cords around my waist.

No, Martin isn't tying me to his bed… sadly. We're in the kitchen because Mr. Posada was hungry, and not for me… this time. He *demanded* my help, hence the apron covering my torso.

"I should be sitting on one of those pretty stools while *you* cook for me."

"I promise this will be more entertaining," he replies.

"I don't think so," I start to say, but he silences me with a scorching kiss. If we continue on this path, breakfast won't be ready anytime soon.

We spent the night entangled with each other. Learning every way to make us surrender to pleasure, seeking new ways to make the other moan—and gasp.

I'm starting to feel dizzy when his lips leave mine and he turns to grab something from the pantry. "What is that?" I scold him, while eyeing the package in his hands. "That isn't Mexican food."

He smirks while placing the pancake mix on the marble counter. "I know how much you love my cock, *cariño*. But we need sustenance." He teases me with a light kiss knowing the effect he has on me. He's not wrong, I am in love with his cock, and all the things he does to me. "And I'll give you more later. Right now, we're making breakfast."

He turns to take out a pan from a drawer.

"You're a millionaire," I tease him with a mocking whine. "Shouldn't you have hired someone to help around the house? Someone to come every time you snap your fingers and keep you fed?"

"Are you applying for the job?" he asks me, looking at me over his shoulder.

Did I mention he's just wearing low hanging, gray sweatpants and nothing else? The way they fit his body should be illegal.

And I know what he is packing underneath.

I'm still standing in the middle of the kitchen while he moves easily around. Getting eggs, milk, and butter from the fridge.

Today, there is no hamper full of my freshly washed clothing so I'm just wearing one of his old t-shirts paired with briefs. I'm a modern girl, but walking naked around the kitchen isn't my idea of comfortable. Even if I'd support the idea of Martin doing it. The man has a body to die for, earlier he told me he works out every day before going to his office. The idea of him lifting while I stretch over my mat on the terrace gives me butterflies.

His phone chimes with an incoming text and Martin smiles while replying.

"Seems like we're gonna have company, *cariño.*" He lifts his gaze to find mine.

"Who?" I reply, my voice full of alarm. I'm not dressed to entertain.

"Gabriel is coming up right now," he says

I panic and run to the room, while Martin's laughter follows me, searching for the dress I was wearing last night. This is so much worse than the walk of shame. Way, way worse.

Where are my panties? No, not the figurative ones, but literally, the lacy pair I was wearing.

Anyway, panties or not, I'm staying in here until Gabriel finds somewhere else to go. It's so inconvenient for me that Erin, as a florist, works most of the weekends.

I hear voices coming from the living area and keep myself busy making the bed. It makes me smile to see the wrinkled sheets. The pillow smells like him. Leather and something mysterious, so delicious. Would it be creepy of me if I stole it? It would pale in comparison as nothing would top him, but a girl's gotta do what she's gotta do.

"Dee," a deep voice calls out my name. "There's no need to hide. I know you're in there."

I'm gonna throttle someone—Martin. I walk toward the kitchen, where they're both leaning against the bar, drinking coffee with identical expressions of mischief plastered on their faces.

"Good morning," Gabriel greets me and Martin snorts. "Such a pleasant surprise to see you, Dee."

"Oh, cut the crap," I sneer at him. "I'm sure you know what's happening here."

"I do," he replies. "But it's fun watching you fight with your embarrassment anyway."

"I'd kick you in the nuts, but I heard my friend is very fond of them."

Gabriel laughs hard and tugs on my hand. "Come here, silly girl. Give me a hug."

"You're the worst," I say but I give him a hug anyway. I've known this man my whole life. There is no malice in his words, just friendly banter.

"That's enough," Martin tugs on me, forcing me to move away from his brother. "Go and fondle your own woman and leave mine alone."

This is new. And I must confess, I like it a lot.

With a smile, I turn to kiss Martin's jaw. "Easy, tiger," I whisper, just loud enough for him to hear.

"I'll show you who's an animal later," he growls back.

We talk for a while, until Martin and his brother finish their coffee. Then Gabriel announces, "Gotta go. See you later, brother."

They hug in the way that men do and then Gabriel's attention turns to me. "Maybe we should go to dinner one of these nights. Come and drive into the city, we'd love to see you."

"We'll see," Martin replies. I know he's doing this for my sake, I was the one who wanted to take this slow."

"Alrighty, selfish man," Gabriel replies, teasing his brother. "Keep her all to yourself. See you at the wedding, Dee."

"I'll be there."

"You better." It's the last thing he says before he closes the door behind him.

"You were so possessive with your brother around," I scold Martin. "Such a caveman."

"Caveman… I thought you said I was a tiger?" he says while prowling toward me, cornering me in the kitchen. Then he proceeds to throw me over his shoulder and spank my ass. "I'll show you caveman."

I kick out, fighting him to put me down. He shows me later how much fun a fight in the sheets could be with his inner caveman and animalistic sexual prowess.

"You, big whore," Monica almost screams while we're taking our lunch break on Monday. I spent the whole weekend with Martin in his apartment. Until I forced him to take me home last night. Staying with him is fun and all, but I still need a bit of space before things become too intense.

Sadly, he didn't fight my decision, just kissed me silly before saying good night. And then nothing—nothing about when we are seeing each other again. Nor a single text today saying how much he wants me, how much he's missing me. *Am I missing him?* Yes. More than I'd like to admit.

I hate this feeling, this uncertainty. I don't want to feel like I'm alone in this. David almost broke my spirit. But Martin, he would shatter my soul.

"You went out with one guy on Friday and ended up spending the night with a different one?" Monica asks in disbelief.

Her face makes me laugh. A mix of pride and envy shine in her green eyes.

"I did," I reply, leaning against the break room counter. Today I'm not wearing my usual nurse uniform, I traded it for dress pants and a silk blouse. Mondays are my day for paperwork. "That wasn't my plan. Gavyn is a good guy, I really wanted to like him."

"But you didn't?"

"No, I didn't." That's my honest reply.

She smiles again. "Could you give me his number?"

"You're crazy."

The receptionist peeks her head out. "Hey, Dee, there's a walk-in, do you have time for her?"

"Sure," I reply, giving my cell phone one last glance. There's a text, of course, but just a silly math joke.

*Martin, why aren't you asking me for a date again? Or an invite over to your place?*

After seeing the patient, organizing the exam rooms, and checking the week's schedule, my shift ends a little later than usual. My feet are killing me, more of a reason not to wear heels anytime soon. I check all the charts, making sure all our reports are uploaded in our data system. All week is fully booked, the supply room needs to be stocked, but I know a new delivery is coming in the morning. With my lab coat hanging from my arm, I open the employee's door, ready to head to my car, when something—or someone—stops me in my tracks.

"You're here?" He's leaning against his car, wearing one hell of a suit.

"Yes, I came to see you," he replies with an impish smile, tugging his hands on the pockets of his tailored pants.

"Me?" I ask him, pointing at my chest. "I don't do booty calls."

I start walking to my car without giving him another glance. Well not a long one. Even if all I want to do is run to him and have those arms around me.

"Did you miss me?"

I give him a death glare. "I didn't."

"Liar," he smiles.

Is it bad I want to smack him?

"What do you want, Martin?"

"To have dinner with you," he replies.

"Oh yeah. You dropped me off at my house last night and today you didn't say a word about tonight. And now you want to have dinner?"

"Why didn't you send me a text, Dee?" he asks. "If you were missing me, why didn't you call?"

"I don't beg for attention," I tell him. At this point I turned to look at him.

"I'm not asking you to beg for anything, *cariño*," he says in a low voice, closing the distance between us. "Why didn't you call?"

I'm incapable of looking him in the eyes. Something inside me is breaking down.

"Were you giving me a way out?" Another question I don't know how to answer. "Were you testing me? Were you testing to see how much I want to be with you?"

He's so close, I can see his leather oxford shoes almost kissing the tip of my heels.

"Are you playing with me?" I manage to ask. "Are you trying to manipulate me into submission?"

"No, baby," he says, taking my head in his hands, forcing me to look into his deep brown eyes. "I sent you several messages all day, even if I was busy, I texted you."

"Why didn't you say something about tonight?" Why am I being so irrational?

"I just wanted to surprise my girl. In time, I hope you'll feel safe and loved, Dee," he replies with so much honesty it leaves me speechless. "Because if it was up to me, I would want you every minute of every single day—I want you with me, always."

"Then you were playing games... I'm not your plaything."

He gives me a light kiss. Just a taste that makes me crave the real thing. "I just wanted to surprise you."

"You certainly did," I whisper. "But I don't like the silence, it makes me uneasy."

"I promise you, Destinee Carr. My silence doesn't mean I'm walking away. It means I'm planning something bigger."

"Yeah. Like a storm, one that's destructive."

"No, baby," he says. "Like love. Because that's what I feel for you."

Then his lips are on mine and I forget why I was so upset. He wants me. The evidence is growing between us.

And somehow that isn't enough.

"Let's have dinner," he says, breaking off the kiss and taking my hand. "I'm starving for dessert."

"You haven't behaved today," I reply. "It's up to me to say whether you deserve a treat."

"Bring it on, *cariño*. Bring it on."

Martin guides me to his car with his hand on mine, I follow him happily. As soon as he opens the door, I notice something on the seat.

"What's this?"

His arms come to circle my waist from behind. "I was thinking of you, Dee."

"Please don't give me the cold shoulder again," I demand. But it's more like a plea.

"Never again," he replies by kissing my neck, giving me chills. "Let's go have dinner before I ravish you."

❋❋❋

"You're such a cheeseball," I accuse him while looking at the red roses in my hands. We're in his car; he's driving with one hand on the wheel and the other holding mine.

"Roses and chocolates, is this' what you regularly bring to dates?"

That makes me smile broadly. No one had given me flowers and sweets before. Not even once.

"Maybe dating you isn't such a bad thing." Teasing him, but my hands are around his arm, with my body leaning into his.

"Dating me will be amazing, Dee. Just wait and see."

He's so sweet, and hot. I've never been with a man like Martin. Like ever.

"Do you think you can take a couple days off before the wedding?" he asks me when we're sitting in a corner booth at a fancy steakhouse, hiding and making out like teenagers.

"Why? Do you have plans?"

He nods. "I was thinking about driving to the resort earlier. It has several private luxury cabins, I'd love to have you to myself for a couple of days. We could go skiing, wine tasting..."

"You had me at luxury..."

Martin smiles, he knows me well. The idea of spending some time with him in a secluded place, the snow... it will be so romantic.

"Do you think you can take the time off?"

"Yeah, it's in my contract. It sounds like fun," I reply. The wedding is three weeks away, it'll be on President's Day weekend.

His eyes light up as he smiles at me, then his attention returns to sign the check the waiter just brought over. "That means you're coming?"

"Well, I hope so," I answer with a wink.

"Often and hard, *cariño,*" he concludes, catching the real meaning of my words.

"Starting tonight?"

"Let's go home," he whispers.

"Yours or mine?"

"Ours," he says as his lips touch mine. Making promises I know he will honor.

# CHAPTER TWENTY

*Destinee*

"This is getting old," Martin says from his place on my bed. He's lounging there looking like a god while I storm around my room picking out some stuff for the next few days. Every time Martin comes to the clinic to pick me up, I end up spending the night at his place. I've learnt to leave some clean clothes at his apartment just in case. While my own home is being neglected, I haven't slept in my bed in the last ten days.

"What are you talking about?"

"You, here packing. This is a waste of time, Dee. Why are you paying rent for a place you never use?"

"Because I can't live in my car." I turn to look at him with my hand on my hips. Is he nuts? "And I signed a lease."

"When are you free of it?"

"April. Why are you asking?"

"I'll cover you until then."

What's happening here, and why am I not following the conversation. "Why? Do you know something I don't know, am I getting fired? I can pay for my own rent, thank you very much. I don't need a sugar daddy."

He gets out of the bed, walking toward me with a predatory look in his eyes. "You can call me daddy anytime you want to, *cariño*. And I'll pour all the sugar on you."

"You're so gross," I pat him on the chest when his arms come around my waist.

"Come on, Dee, say you'll move in with me."

I blink a couple times, as if that makes me hear better.

"What? Are you crazy?"

"Why not?" he asks, like the answer was so simple. But it's not, the matter is very complicated.

Martin has lost his freaking mind. I can't move in with him. "First off… as I said, I have my own place, and it so happens that I like it."

He makes a face. Of course I'm lying about this one.

"Secondly," I say, counting with my fingers. "You haven't asked…"

Martin smiles at me, and I swear my panties disintegrate. The man's smile is lethal, and he knows it.

"What do you think I'm trying to do, Destinee?"

The arms around my waist tighten, but I use mine to make space between us.

"I haven't finished," I say, this one will be painful to say but it's the most important. "My final point is that I know I'm your little secret, Martin. But I understand why, honestly."

Something inside me breaks a bit, but I get it. As soon as his family knows about us, it will be a huge issue. I'm sure David never loved me, but he's stubborn, and prideful. And there is nothing as dangerous as an arrogant man with his ego bruised.

"What are you talking about?" he asks me with wide eyes and his brow lifted. "Gabriel knows about us."

Well, nothing new there, Gabriel and Martin are like two peas in a pod. They know everything about each other.

The other day we had dinner with him and Erin. Both of them seem fine with our relationship, and my bets are Gabriel briefed his fiancée beforehand. We had a great time, as if this new situation were completely normal, and not a thing in the gray area, turning into forbidden territory.

I love it when he holds my hand, and the way he's always touching me. Martin always leans in his chair to be closer to me. Cuddles me every night, and in the mornings, always brings me a cup of coffee before going for a run.

He makes me believe. However, the little voice is still there, hidden in a corner of my mind, murmuring nasty things like I don't deserve this. Like I wasn't made for Martin to love me, or any other man. Like I'd always be begging for crumbs of love. Because I'm not worth more.

I work to better myself every day, but old habits are hard to break. Even when you have the most wonderful boyfriend in the entire world. Martin knows about my insecurities, and helps me to feel cherished all the time. He gives me his time, his undivided attention. He makes plans and always discusses them with me. He includes me in everything, because my feelings matter to him.

Martin kisses me softly, figuring out where my thoughts are at. "Dee, I want to tell my father and Lena after the wedding. I was thinking about talking to them on Sunday, after the newlyweds leave for their honeymoon."

That makes sense. We won't steal their thunder, and just in case David decides to throw a tantrum, only the family will be there.

"What do you think?"

"It sounds like a plan." A smile pulls at my lips and his does the same.

"And what if we spend the holiday with your parents? Will we tell them by then?"

This is as serious as a heart attack. Well not literally, but this is an attack on my heart, nonetheless.

"Do you think your family will be supportive?" he asks, his eyes full of concern. "I know they never approved…"

I know but I don't want to go there.

"My mother will be elated," I tell him. She will be over the moon. "She was always clear and *very* loud about me falling in love with the wrong brother."

His smile turns wider. "Oh yeah?"

I roll my eyes. "Don't play coy, Martin Posada, you know my mother loves you."

"Will your father chase me with his shotgun?"

"Probably," I'm telling the truth. "But he won't kill you and your balls are safe. They want grandkids one day."

He pushes me against his body playfully. "Are you thinking of having kids already?"

Just the thought terrifies me, to be honest.

"Let's get this move-in-with-me matter figured out first, shall we?"

He smiles. Knowing Martin, the wheels inside his head are in motion already.

"I'll send the movers tomorrow."

No, no, that's way too soon. I need to talk with Crystal about this first.

"Hold your horses." Then an idea comes to my mind. "I think we should wait until we come back from the wedding and see how it goes, don't you?"

"Why do you want to waste more time?"

No, I don't want to waste more time... I just want to feel... like this isn't breakable.

Martin is a force of nature, and I'm... well, I'm me. The girl who's starting to believe in herself.

"At least tell me you're staying at home every night." I love the way he refers to his apartment as home. Not my house or something.

Martin is the most generous guy I've ever known.

"Maybe we should stay here tonight," I tease him.

"Dee, I need space, I'm a big boy." Oh yes, he's a *big boy* indeed. "That bed is just a full-size."

"You'll fit," I reply with a smirk.

"As I fit perfectly inside you, *cariño?*"

His words whispered in my ear makes me hornier by the second. He's so cocky. And has all the reasons to be... the man came well-equipped to make a girl happy. Plus, he knows how to use his tools.

"Don't be wicked," I scold him with a soft pat on his hard chest.

"You're asking for the impossible," he replies, then lets me go. "If you want to stay here tonight, then we're staying here. After, we're packing a bag for the next few days, you can even bring your dirty clothes and all."

"Is that a ruse to get your way with me in the laundry room?"

Martin smacks my ass. "You mean again, right?"

He took care of that as soon as the opportunity presented itself. His washer is so big for me to sit on top of it, but he chose to fuck me so hard from behind, I could barely walk the next day. It was so spontaneous and thrilling.

"Are you remembering, dirty girl?"

I just shrug in response, I need to finish packing all my clothes.

"You want me to beg you?"

Another smug smile… this guy. "There is no need to beg for what's yours, baby. But I like to look at you on your knees."

His words make the pulse between my legs intensify. I close the distance between us, my hand on his zipper, ready to act. The bulge inside his pants is begging for my attention. My mouth waters at the thought.

Feeling Martin come undone and under my control makes me feel powerful. It doesn't matter if I'm on my knees. I'm still in charge.

"Seems like you need me right now…"

"I always need you, *cariño.*" His voice comes out strangled, as if he were in pain.

"What do you want, Martin?"

He takes a pillow from the bed and throws it at my feet.

He always thinks of my well-being first. All the time.

"On your knees, Destinee," he orders, and I fall in front of him willingly. "Put those pretty lips around my cock."

"Baby, some people I want to do business with are coming from Germany to New York next week. Wanna come with me?"

We are about to have dinner. The lady who delivers food came earlier today with a fresh batch of *cochinita pibil*—a Mexican pork dish—and we found everything ready to have dinner on the terrace when we arrived a few minutes ago.

"Next week?" I shriek, my voice like nails on a chalkboard. It's Thursday, we have plans for next week. We're driving to Lake Tahoe to spend a few days before the wedding in a cabin.

"I'm flying out on Sunday night and coming back on Tuesday morning," he replies easily. "I haven't forgotten about the plans we made, Dee."

Valentine's Day is this Monday, I want to pout. He's inviting me to come, though. My manager at the clinic was very gracious when I asked him for three days off, but I don't think he will be happy if on top of that I ask for the entire week off.

"I can't, Martin." New York with him sounds heavenly, but this girl wants to keep her job. "My boss…"

"Are you sure?" He takes my hand and kisses me on the palm.

I want to scream, but I bite my tongue and manage an answer. "I am. I'll miss you, though."

"And I'll miss you, baby."

"Buy a souvenir for me, ok?" That's my attempt to set myself at ease, but my heart is sinking. I wanted to celebrate our first Valentine's Day together. And he's forgotten about it, or maybe the lover's holiday wasn't even on his radar.

I was hoping for the cheesy stuff. Dinner and red roses. Heart-shaped balloons and chocolates. I organized a night for the both of us. A few days ago, I went to an exclusive lingerie store and bought the most beautiful set of panties and bustier in a deep shade of red. What else could I give to the man who owns the world, other than myself?

"I will," he says and rewards me with a smile. "You stay here, Gabriel knows I'm leaving and he will be in touch in case you need something."

"Martin, I'm not a child. Everything will be fine." My voice sounds sour but he ignores my tone and keeps talking as if I said nothing. "I'll be back on Tuesday and then we are leaving for our getaway, ok?"

"Ok," I agreed in an attempt to change the subject. To make this situation lighter. "The food is getting cold."

After dinner, as soon as we make it into the bedroom, he undresses me slowly. Kisses me hard and makes love to me with infinite patience. Telling me how much I mean to him, how much he wants me. How much he will miss me while he's away.

But inside me something is breaking.

Something is telling me the pattern is repeating itself.

# CHAPTER TWENTY-ONE

*Destinee*

"How are you feeling about this?" Crystal, my therapist, asks me. I requested an extra session for this week. The only time she was available was around lunch on Monday. So this time I'm stuck in my office, almost whispering every word.

"He forgot about today. My brain understands he's working, but in my heart, I feel like he left me behind again."

"Did you talk about this with him?"

"No," I quickly reply. "What kind of bitch would that make me? He's working Crystal, working."

I look at the white walls of my small office, trying to get my shit together.

"Destinee, therapy won't give you all the magic answers. I'm here just to provide you with the tools to cope with the situations you might find yourself in. Relationships require work, and communication. You need to learn to trust him and talk about what's bothering you."

Yesterday, I woke up in his arms. Warm and happy, then reality came crashing down like an avalanche. He packed his bags while I was sitting on the bed incapable of saying a word. He asked me several times what's wrong, but I managed to divert his attention by saying I'll miss him.

Today our bed was cold and lonely. I slept hugging his pillow, but it was a cold reminder he is on the other side of the country.

He called me as soon as the plane landed last night and then again when he was alone in his room. The chance to sext was wasted, because I wasn't in the mood. And this morning when I opened my eyes, a message was waiting for me. Martin was leaving for his business meeting, and he just wanted me to know he may be far away but that he left his heart in my hands.

"Destinee, falling in love is just the beginning." Crystal continues, those words shake me to my core like an earthquake. Love. I'm in love, I'm pretty sure of it. And terrified about it. "Making it last is the real challenge."

"I don't know what to do." I feel weak admitting it out loud.

"I think a good start would be to talk with him," she says. "You told me you both are leaving for a romantic getaway this week. That offers you the perfect opportunity to talk to him about your fears. Maybe he'll surprise you,

Destinee. Cut the man some slack, he seems really devoted to you."

He really is. Martin is amazing in every way.

"I'll talk to him, I promise."

We keep chatting for a while. Crystal never sugarcoats anything, she tells me whatever is on her mind as is. Maybe that's the reason I like her so much, she pushes my boundaries.

On my way home, I decide to make a quick stop at the liquor store and treat myself to an expensive bottle of wine. If Martin forgot about Valentine's Day, this will remind him, and we'll celebrate over the phone—or FaceTiming. It will be fun either way.

Suddenly the idea of being at home alone doesn't seem so dreadful. I'll shower and dress in the lingerie I bought. My heart is pounding hard against my ribs at the very thought. I'm excited, so eager to talk with him.

*Get ready, Martin Posada, tonight will be a great night for us. It will be special, even if you're on the other side of the country.*

His apartment is dark, which is odd because Martin developed a system to turn on all the lights when someone commands. It's like a very specialized type of Siri, but this one is called Tom and just answers at the sound of his voice. Or mine.

"Tom, turn the lights on," I command, but the lights remain off.

Fuck, something isn't right. Why doesn't this man have security around? Do I need a bodyguard or something?

Then I feel a breeze, as if the terrace doors were open.

Someone is here to kill me.

## *Martin*

I'm on my terrace wearing one of my best suits, it's black and fitted with a white crisp shirt sans tie, waiting for Destinee to walk outside, with the hope she approves. Through the security cameras in the garage, I watch her park her car and then enter the apartment. The sun has set, and the night is softly illuminated by the glow of a ton of candles around.

"Happy Valentine's Day, *cariño,*" I tell her at the exact moment her eyes open wide, and her jaw falls in shock.

I had a surprise waiting for her. A table for two, red roses, and what I expect is the perfect gift. After a short trip across the country this seems even sweeter.

It wasn't easy, believe me. Destinee is transparent, my girl's face hides nothing. As soon as I told her about my business trip, disappointment was written all over her gorgeous features. I wanted to hug her and tell her I hadn't forgotten about our first Valentine's Day but knowing a bigger reward was on the way, I kept up the façade.

"I thought someone was here to kill me," she says in an exasperated voice, but a small smile is pulling up those lips I'm dying to kiss.

"Aren't you happy to see me?"

Dee flies into my arms, I'm ready to catch her and hug her tightly.

"I missed you so much," she whispers between kisses.

"I missed you more." She looks gorgeous, her glorious curves draped in a black dress paired with red heels. My mouth waters at the sight of her body.

"And I thought…"

"I know," I chuckle in response.

"You played me," she fake scolds me, but I know how happy she is about me being here tonight. My plan was to make her feel special. I know my girl, I know she wants the full romantic experience. Destinee has dreamt of the typical fairy tale all her life. From afar, I watched her swoon when my sister fell in love with her husband. Not because she wanted Cardan for herself, but because she wanted to be the heroine in her own love story.

"No, baby, I just wanted to make it special for you."

"I don't care," she replies. "I just wanted you here."

"And here I am."

"Tell me everything," she urges. "Tell me everything and then take me to bed."

"Aren't you hungry?" I counter. "Dinner is waiting for us."

"Dinner?"

I just smile, before kissing her quickly. "Come with me." With my arm around her I guide her to the table I set for two.

Destinee melts at the sight before her. The girl I hired did an amazing job, our terrace was transformed into the perfect oasis for two tonight. It's amazing what you're able to do with unlimited resources at one's disposal.

"You did this for us?"

"No, *cariño,* I did all of this for you."

"You're the boyfriend of the year," she cries out.

"Just of the year?" I tease her. "I'm sorely disappointed."

"You don't need more fuel for your ego," her voice is still playful and happy. "You know you're the only one for me."

Well, that's the best gift a guy can get from the woman he loves.

Yes, I'm in love with her. I always have been.

And always will be.

I kiss her again, my cock between us is so hard and ready for her. But that isn't how I planned for the night to go. Dinner first, then dessert.

Dee's tummy makes a funny noise and embarrassment covers her face. "I didn't get the chance to grab something for lunch." I pull out her chair for her to sit and then do the same in front of her. "How was New York?"

"It went well." My trip was important for my company. One of my short-term goals is to expand overseas, and this German company is looking for a new partner. I'm ready to jump in. We had a dinner meeting last night and one more meeting at breakfast this morning. After all we'd discussed, Finnegan Barnes, my associate, stayed and was ready to iron out the details and sign the deal. My attendance was no longer required. I hopped back on the private plane, eager to get back to the woman I love.

"Are you planning another trip anytime soon?" she asks me with her blue eyes full of excitement.

"Why? Ready to catch a flight to Munich?"

"Always," she says with a wink.

"Maybe in the summer."

Destinee smiles. "That would be easier if you weren't like a grasshopper, always jumping from one place to the other."

I just smile, but without agreeing. I want to take her around the globe with me, but she has a job she loves, and I must respect that.

"I made plans of my own," she says after a while. The paella the catering company made for us is delicious. The next time we will be here celebrating, all of our family will be here surrounding us, hiring them again sounds like a good idea.

"Oh, yeah?"

"Yep," she nods. "I splurged on a really expensive bottle of red, so I'd be ready to FaceTime and celebrate with you tonight."

"Where is it? You want some?" Right now we're drinking Dom Perignon and our flutes are half empty, but if Dee is in the mood for wine…

"This bubbly is delicious, and we are celebrating. We can drink the bottle of wine over the weekend."

"Everything is all set?"

She makes a noise of excitement. This little getaway of ours will be enlightening for us. Not only will it be our first vacation together, but we'll be announcing our relationship to our families.

As soon as I take the dishes to the kitchen and the table is cleared, I take her to one of the outdoor sofas. There's a gas heater above us making the temperature perfect. I'm dying to get my hands on her. And, of course, to give her the little gift I have in store for her.

I take the velvet box from the interior pocket of my suit jacket and place it on her lap. She gasps. Yeah, it's jewelry. Not the kind which means more. But it's a big gesture anyway. Walking around the store was a new experience for me, not having a clue about what to buy, until the moment my eyes found the earrings.

"Oh my gosh, Martin," she says after opening the lid. "This is too much."

"No more beautiful than you." The diamonds are shining under the lights, but nothing eclipses the spark in her eyes.

"Dragonflies. You're far too generous, thank you." Her fingertips are softly touching the strands of little diamonds.

"I thought these would look good with your dress for the wedding." At this moment, I still feel like I'm the nerd running around her with a book tucked under his arm and a fishing rod in hand.

"I'd rather have your arms around me all the time," she says. "But I understand, we will be together all the time anyway, right?"

"Damn right," I nod. I'm not letting her out of my sight for a second.

"And I have a little something for you too..." she adds. "Not as extravagant as diamond earrings, but..."

"You thought of me, baby. That's the only thing I need." I pull her onto my lap, I'm tired of having so much distance between us.

"It's in the bedroom," she whispers.

"I don't want to sound like an ungrateful motherfucker, but you feel too good grinding over my lap to let you go."

"It's something lacy," the vixen says, smiling at me wickedly. "And strappy."

"And I hope you aren't very fond of it, because my bets are it won't last a minute before I rip it to shreds."

"It's your gift," she grins. "You may do whatever you please with it."

This is a tough decision for me, she looks pretty excited about it. As much as I want to keep her on my lap, I'll let her go to give me her surprise.

"You have five minutes," I inform her. "Starting now."

While she runs to our room, I take the time to turn the heater off and to refill the ice bucket. This champagne will be perfect to quench our thirst once we're both sated. There's also a box full of chocolate covered strawberries waiting for us in the fridge that we can enjoy with it.

With all the stuff in hand, I head slowly toward the room, even if all I want is to run to her.

I stand motionless once my eyes find Destinee standing at the foot of the bed, a red rose dangling from her fingers and her body covered in what I could only describe as a few scraps of lace that leaves nothing to the imagination. My gaze takes her in from head to toe, as I command her, "Don't move." Without taking my eyes off of her, I walk past the foot of the bed to set the items I'm holding on the bedside table. This gives me the chance to appreciate my gift from behind.

"Come here," I say while sitting on the bed.

Her arms loop around my neck, pulling me close. Her legs between mine. My hands creep up her soft thighs, feeling the lacy fabric of her lingerie.

"You take my breath away," I whisper, tracing the hem of her barely-there-panties. "You do it every day."

I remove her bra from her body. I never was a boob man until hers. Those twin peaks are round, soft, and the perfect handful. And her nipples taste so exquisite.

"Thank you," she smiles. "I can't believe a guy like you has eyes for a girl like me."

"Why wouldn't I?" The question leaves my mouth and at the same time, my gaze looms over hers. "You're… Beautiful. Caring. Smart. Why is that so hard to believe?"

"You make me feel that way every time we are together."

"You should feel that way all the time, because you are all of that and more. It doesn't matter if we're together or not."

She blinks a couple times as if processing what I just said.

"I love you, Martin," she murmurs, her fingers are softly massaging my scalp.

"Good," I reply.

Her hands stop their ministrations.

"Good?" she asks with a hint of surprise and indignation in her voice.

"Yeah, good," I smirk. "Because I love you too, Destinee Carr."

"Do you really?" she sounds shocked, but I'm not interested in arguing, not when she's here looking this way.

My mouth has better things to do, like licking its way across her flat stomach and then south to the sweet place between her legs.

From above, I hear her whimper and protest a little when I tear her panties from her body. She doesn't need to worry, I'll buy her the entire store if that makes her happy. Setting her on the bed I part her legs and bury my face at her core. She's wet and warm and delicious. I feel ravenous for her, I lick and suck, torturing her with my tongue. Teasing her clit with a slow, sensual pattern. She tastes even better than any dessert.

Her hands are clawing at the sheets, when my fingers slip inside her, I can feel her muscles spasming and her body is beginning to tense up. Moving faster and harder, pushing her a little more over the edge. My cock is so jealous, and ready to join the party... Suddenly Dee is crying out my name in elation, her orgasm like waves, pulsing from her body into mine.

"I need your cock—now," she says in a mellow, sated voice.

"Are you ready for it?"

"Always."

I've never removed my clothing so quickly before. I tear and pull and throw without a care in the world.

I brace myself over her and in one single thrust enter her sweet body. Beneath me, I watch Destinee's expression, her eyes closing as she adjusts to the size of me. Her breathing becomes more labored when I start to move.

"Oh God. Don't stop," she urges me. Her hands are going down my back, as I follow her command. "Give me what's mine."

I keep moving, in long deep strokes that make her back arch. And her fingers bite into my skin, marking me. I planned to go slow with her, to savor her sweetness all night long, but I find myself struggling for control.

The way she moves doesn't help. She urges me with her hands. With those tempting kisses, and whispers in my ear about how much she loves me.

I'm doomed. So fucking close…

"Martin, make me come," she moans. "Fuck me like you mean it. And don't stop."

*Mierda.* Fuck. After hearing those dirty words coming from her sweet lips the caveman inside me is unleashed. Groaning, I begin to move again, harder this time. Giving my girl exactly what she asked for. The bed starts to bang against the wall, I'm glad I don't have any neighbors. With my eyes closed, I hear her crying out and finally feel her clenching around me, setting off my own release.

Giving her everything while we both explode in hot, warm waves of relief.

I fall to the side, taking her with me. Our skin slick with sweat, the smell of sex floating in the air around us.

Her hand strokes my chest, while mine roams up and down her back, my lips in her hair. Eventually, she lifts her head enough to look at me.

"I really love you, Martin." I'm pretty sure I'll never get tired of hearing those words.

"I love you, Dee."

"Is this real?"

"It is," I smile at her. But her gaze is fearful.

"I need to tell you something," she breathes deeply. "I had an extra session with Crystal today."

"About what?" It's my turn to be nervous.

"Because my feelings were eating away at me. Because my fear was bigger than I could handle. Because I'm so in love with you that if you leave me, I know it will break me."

*Oh, mi amor. My sweet love.* "You need to know I plan to spend my whole life with you." She needs to know I'm serious about us. "Also, you're stronger than you think, Destinee. You will stay standing, no matter what, you will survive."

She takes another gulp of air. "There is something you don't know and that's…" Her eyes start to water. What the fuck is happening?

"You can tell me when you're ready, ok? And I'll be here to listen."

She closes her eyes and nods. Her mouth set in a sad line.

"Now, come here." I hug her harder, tighter. She's in my heart, in my soul, in every cell of my body. "This, between us, is the real deal, Destinee."

"Yes," she whispers in agreement, hanging onto my body like a lifeline. "We are the real deal."

# CHAPTER TWENTY-TWO

*Destinee*

"Pinch me, I think I'm dreaming."

Martin comes from behind me as I lean over the edge of the hot tub and places a kiss on my bare shoulder. "I'll gladly pinch you anywhere you want."

I start giggling, but my giggle turns into a moan when his hands cup my boobs. His mouth is on my neck, tempting me. Making me melt.

This is our second day at the resort. We're in our little cabin-in-the-woods, and the view is breathtaking. I want to stay here forever. And I mean in his arms. It's the best place on Earth to be.

This is what being in love means. I wake up everyday with a smile on my face and my heart fluttering. Sadly, our little bubble for two is about to burst. Today, Martin's family will arrive among the other wedding guests. This isn't just a function, it's a big celebration. It starts on Thursday night, runs all day Friday, and then into the actual wedding on

Saturday, followed by a breakfast on Sunday. Martin invited his father to stay another day to rest after the festivities, then Cardan announced they are doing the same, and therefore, the whole Posada bunch is staying until Monday. This gives us the perfect time to announce our relationship. Martin made reservations at a private dining room, and everything is all set. My man does everything big, and I love him for that. With every step we move forward I feel reassured, and that's what I need. My heart is still healing and my soul is starting to learn the art of believing.

But we have a few more hours until then. My plan is to live them to the fullest.

"What are you thinking about?"

"I want us to live together," I reply, my gaze wandering to the lake in front of us.

The path of his mouth on my skin stops. "I thought we had that settled."

I turn to look at him. "No," I say. "I really want to live with you, Martin. I don't care if we stay at your apartment, a cabin in the mountains, or a shack by the river. I *really* want to be with you."

The chocolate of his eyes melts at my words. God, he's so gorgeous. And all mine.

My hands travel from the hard expanse of his chest to his shoulders.

"I think we should celebrate," he whispers with a wicked glint glimmering in his dark pupils.

The hot water is bubbling around us, but it feels like the snow around the cabin defrosted and summer is heating our entwining bodies.

"Take me to the bedroom." I'm so ready for him, my entire being aches to feel him again.

"No, I want you here," he replies.

"Outside?" Oh my God…

"You have to stay very quiet, if you don't want the entire resort to know how hard I'm fucking you."

Martin whirls me around onto his lap so I'm straddling him and he starts tugging at the strings of my bikini bottom. Then his fingers are tangled at the nape of my neck, yanking me down in the most intense kiss. The hot water and the vapor around us like a cocoon, prolonging our time.

I'm an idiot, all these years wasted because I clung desperately to an impossibility when the perfect man for me was waiting right here. David didn't break my heart; I did that to myself. Maybe I was trying to channel all the feelings my heart had in store for Martin into David. Martin was always the one for me, the only one who listened when everyone else was bored of my shenanigans. The man who's patient enough to wait for my brain to catch up with my heart.

Maybe this was written in our stars. Destined to be.

His hands are extended on my back while his mouth works lower to my breasts while my fingers tug on his hair. The scratch of his teeth over my sensitive nipple sends an electric shock of desire across my veins.

The black fabric of my bikini still clinging between us, torturing me with all his skills. But I'm beyond foreplay. Not when this throbbing ache for him is consuming me.

I shift in his lap, looking for his hard cock and slipping it between my folds. This time I yank him into my kiss. Claiming him. My entire body is trembling for him, the emotions are overwhelming. And empowering. Martin is allowing me to control what's happening here, not because he's sitting and I'm on top, but he's allowing me to grow. To fly.

Neither of us are gonna last. And I can't hold on, it's too intense. Each thrust claims me over and over again. I'm pretty sure my nails will leave marks on his bronzed skin, and he will definitely love that.

The bikini top is pushing my breasts together and Martin takes the chance to ravish them. My heart is beating so hard, he should feel it. I'm so fucking close and he's right there, at the edge with me.

Martin drives into me, in a final thrust that makes us fall over. But I'm not just falling, I'm soaring as bliss fills every cell in my body and makes it impossible to find oxygen to breathe. My mouth hangs open and I can barely make a sound. My eyes are closed and my arms wrap around his neck.

"God, I love you," he grunts against my heaving chest.

"I love you," I pant in answer.

"I can't wait to announce to the world that you're mine and stop with all this hiding bullshit."

That burst the bubble. "Umm... About that, I'm going to my room tonight."

"The hell you are," he replies, untangling himself from my grasp.

"Martin, it's for the best. I don't want anyone to see me here with you and..."

He looks into my eyes. "You stay here. I upgraded your room when I checked in, so I'll take it. It's not like I'm going to sleep anyway."

Even if I'm smiling, worry is filling me. "What would I say if they ask? Your family knows I don't have the means to pay for this."

"If someone asks, tell them to shut the fuck up."

"Martin..." It's impossible to argue with him when his blood is already boiling. He's so stubborn. And determined.

"Fine," he accepts. "We can tell everyone that I'm just being a gentleman and you would be more comfortable in the cabin."

"Martin, I've seen pictures. All the rooms here are top-notch."

"You're staying here," he states, leaving no room for argument. "The only people whose opinion I give a shit about is my family, and soon enough they'll know you're mine."

My mother always called me hardheaded, but even I know when to stop in an argument. And I'm not winning this one.

✻✻✻

Cardan, Elena, and her father are the first to arrive. We are lounging in the bistro bar when they enter and greet us happily.

"Oh my," I tell Lena. "You're—"

"As huge as a house," she cuts me off before I have the chance to end the sentence.

"I was about to say glowing," I correct her. "Pregnancy is doing wonders for you, my friend."

"I tell her the same thing every day," says Cardan, before kissing my cheek. "This one has been so moody lately…"

That earns him a poke to the ribs.

"That has nothing to do with the pregnancy," Martin adds from behind me and Lena gives him a killer glare. "How are things going?" He asks Cardan as they shake hands.

"The same old story, *hermano.*" I love how Cardan is now one of them, even attempting to speak a little Spanish. To his credit he doesn't sound like Diego from *Dora the Explorer* or anything.

Ignacio, Martin's father, comes to greet us too. And sits in one of the upholstered chairs.

"Silicon Valley suits you, Dee. You look happier than the last time we talked." Mr. Posada says with contentment in his voice. The man is like a father to me. I hope one day we make it official. I'd love to be one of them.

"As do you, Mr. Posada. Is Lena finally giving you a break?"

He smiles at me, with the corners of his dark eyes wrinkling. "I hope one day soon you will call me *papá*, as all my kids do."

My shocked gaze seeks Martin immediately, who's looking at me like a hawk, but none of us say a word. And I don't have the chance to ask Mr. Posada for more because Gabriel and Erin enter the room followed by Ruben and David.

We all sit around a big coffee table and start chatting about the plans for the upcoming days. Martin and I are in separate chairs, with the way he's leaning against the furniture I can tell he's itching to touch me.

"Are you coming skiing with us tomorrow after breakfast, *papá?*" Gabriel asks. "The girls are spending the day at the spa with Erin."

"Someone has to show you how it's done," Mr. Posada replies playfully. "All these years and my boys haven't learned yet."

I swear the four of them groan and Lena grins. "I'm the only one who bears the family last name proudly."

"Baby, your last name is Malone now," Cardan reminds her.

"Whatever," my friend replies but Cardan ignores her and kisses her hand.

"Then it's settled," Ruben announces, rubbing his hands together. "We're going to hit the slopes tomorrow."

"After that they'll be waiting on us at the barbershop." Gabriel adds.

"And I thought Erin was the scheduling patrol," Martin says, winking at his future sister-in-law.

She points at him with her finger. "Watch your mouth, Martin."

"Ooh. We're starting to rub off on you," he concludes with a laugh. Erin has changed a lot in the last couple of years, the shy girl who Gabriel brought to the orchard is long gone.

"My parents are about to arrive," she says standing. "We're having dinner together."

"It's all in the schedule," David speaks for the first time since he arrived. His intense gaze on me, as if he were looking for an answer to an unspoken question.

It doesn't matter. I'm beyond that.

"What's happening?" Lena asks me after a while, when she drags me to the balcony for a little private chat. "Something is happening between my brother and you."

"Nothing is happening between David and I, and you know it," I try to dismiss her.

She gives me the mother of all eye rolls. "I'm not stupid, Dee. Martin and you are together now, aren't you?"

My heart stops. "Is it that obvious?"

She grins like the cat that got the cream. "I knew it," she says, jumping up and down. "I told Cardan the first time you were home weeks ago. You were like tied by an invisible force, and it's exploding."

"Are you mad?" My hands are gripping the iron rail in front of me, I don't care if it's freezing. I need some support to keep me standing.

"Why would I be?" she replies, her eyes full of understanding.

"I don't know… because I'm getting with all your brothers?"

She laughs. "Erin would have an issue with that, if that's your plan. But seriously, we all knew Martin has been in love with you since fucking forever. It was about time you realized it. David never deserved you, Dee. How you managed to stay with him for so many years is beyond my comprehension."

*Believe me, sister, beyond mine too.*

I turn to look at her with a small smile. "We're announcing it on Sunday, at the family dinner. We don't want to steal Gabriel and Erin's thunder."

"I'm sure they won't care."

"They won't," I blurt out.

"I'm gonna kill you. Don't tell me Erin knew about this before me. I thought I was your best friend."

I hug her. "You're the best in the world. But everything happened so fast, between work and therapy, I'm just catching up. I promise I'll call you next week and tell you everything."

"You better," she points at me with her finger and at the same moment Cardan pokes his head through the door.

"What are you doing here? It's freezing and I don't want you to catch a cold."

"We're coming," she says and she starts walking to the bar, but not without giving me the stink eye.

Gah, I've missed my bestie so much.

# CHAPTER TWENTY-THREE

*Martin*

"I was missing you," Destinee whispers sleepily while I sneak into the bed behind her. I'm naked and primed. She's so fucking perfect, all soft and warm, I bet if I slid my fingers in her pussy, I'll find her ready for me.

This is our second night in *separate* rooms. Well, at least my luggage is in the other room, there is no way I'm letting her sleep alone. She's mine. We belong together. I stay wherever she stays. Period.

"Well, I'm here now," I reply, kissing the nape of her neck, her shoulder blades and moving lower.

"How did it go with your father?"

After the rehearsal dinner ended, my father pulled me aside. He wanted to have a word with me alone. *Papá* knows me well, better than myself, it's impossible for me to hide something from him. Let alone my feelings for Dee.

"He's worried about David's reaction," I confess, while my lips are still wandering across her silky skin.

"He knows about us too?" she cries out and pushes up on her elbows lifting her body from the bed.

"Too?" I ask. "Who else knows?"

"Elena," she confesses in a sigh. "It seems like we aren't as sneaky as we thought."

"I know my sister's opinion matters to you."

"Your father's too," she adds. "What did he say?"

"My father loves you like a daughter," I remind her what she already knows. "He's just concerned about David. He was wasted tonight."

That's true, my brother drank a lot tonight. By the time the evening ended, Ruben had to drag him out of the room before he embarrassed himself in front of Gabriel's guests.

"I'm worried about him too." She turns on the bed to look at me. The curtains are open, and the moon is lighting up the room with a soft glow. "He's acting weird, do you think he's in trouble?"

As a man, I'm jealous about her concern for him. But as David's brother I must say I'm worried too.

"*Papá* is going to talk to him tomorrow after breakfast," I say, pulling the sheet lower. I want to see more of her. Destinee is wearing a lace slip that leaves very little to the imagination. And believe me. Every time we are in the same room—and even if we aren't—mine is working overtime.

"Seems like the family dinner will be more like a formality." She doesn't know it, but I have a surprise in store for her. The dragonfly earrings weren't the only thing I bought at the jewelry store in New York. I'm so ready to move forward with our relationship. I can't wait for it.

"Do you want me to cancel it?" I ask but inside my mind I'm begging her to say no.

"No," she whispers when I bite one of her pebbled nipples. "I want to…"

"I'm willing to give you whatever you want, but now, the time to talk is over."

I push my body between her legs and for a long time the room is filled with the sounds of our bodies colliding.

✳✳✳

Weddings are like the twilight zone for me. Uncharted territory. But sitting here with the woman I've loved for as long as I can remember by my side, all I can think of is I want this for us. Maybe in milder weather for a change. I'm freezing my ass off.

While my brother promises to love and cherish his bride for as long as he lives my body is craving to take Destinee between my arms and dry those tears she's shedding.

"Fuck it," I whisper before twining her fingers with mine. If someone wants to talk, I don't give a shit about it.

Her beautiful eyes open in shock, but she doesn't say a word, just holds my hand tighter.

I've missed her so much, it's like we haven't had the chance to see each other, it feels like a decade. Destinee has been running around with Erin and my sister dealing with the wedding prep while I follow Gabriel around town.

And speaking of my older brother, he's standing at the altar with his wife-to-be looking cool and composed. His hands are steady while she looks at him with complete adoration. My father, on the other hand, is a mess. He's sitting beside an empty chair with a lone white rose over it. It was the same at Elena's wedding. My father tried to keep it together while missing the woman he promised to love forever. Seeing him so undone cements my decision. Life is too short for us to waste it. I'm determined to spend all my days with Dee.

When the minister announces they are married and everyone around us stands and claps, my father takes the flower with him. I know what it means. My heart breaks for him a little more. Fucking life is so unfair sometimes. My mother should be here sharing this happy memory with us. Lena will become a mother in a couple of months, and she won't be there to meet her first grandchild or be able to give my sister advice.

"One day we will do all of this for you," Erin says to Destinee when we approach the newlywed couple to congratulate them.

Dee says nothing but gives me a small smile and a shy glance. *Yes, baby, one day we will do all of this.*

"She looks gorgeous, doesn't she?" Destinee says when we follow the newlyweds to the place the photographer is waiting for us to take the family photos.

"She does," I agree. "By the way, you look stunning."

It's true. The sapphire blue of her dress makes her eyes even brighter and her hair is styled curlier making Dee way sexier. The fabric goes to her feet, but with every step a long slit gives me a peek of her legs and my mouth waters. And not to mention the backless detail of her dress... I've been fighting a hard-on since she arrived at the patio where the ceremony was taking place.

"Thank you," she whispers. "I can't wait to get you all to myself."

"Later." That's a promise I intend to fulfill. Like all the promises I've made to her.

"In the meantime, are you ready to show me your best moves?"

"Haven't I, already?" I give her a wicked smile.

And she rewards me with an eye roll. "Is your mind always in the gutter?"

I don't add another word, just place her little hand on my arm and continue walking.

My father has given his speech, dinner was served, and the band is playing upbeat songs while the dance floor is full of people. Us among them. Destinee loves to dance and I'm happy to give my girl whatever she wants even if I need to keep my hands from going too low across her back.

I'm nursing a beer with Gabriel while Lena and Dee assist Erin in the ladies' room when Cardan comes to sit with us.

"Don't you think David is drinking a little bit too much tonight?"

As if we've summoned it, my father stands from his place alongside my aunts to check on my brother.

Fucking David. This childish attitude is pissing me off.

From the moment he arrived at the resort, I've felt his eyes following Destinee everywhere. He's glaring if my hands touch her… If she talks with me his gaze is on us. And yes, my girl and I have spent a hell of a lot of time together.

"*Papá* is worried," Gabriel says while the three of us look at my father who's talking to David.

"Elena too," Cardan adds. "And I hate seeing her so upset these days. This should be a happy time for her."

"I don't want Destinee to feel guilty about this," I tell both of them.

"No one is blaming Dee for his actions, Tin," my brother tells me.

"Are you sure?" I counter with lifted brows.

"That relationship was doomed from the very beginning," Gabriel says and then sips his bourbon. "If there's one fault Dee has, it's that she stayed with him for so many years."

"She's staying away from him now," I say in my girl's defense. She's not here to speak up for herself.

"And here comes my wife," Gabriel announces with his voice full of pride.

"I'm exhausted," my sister cries out as soon as she is beside Cardan. "Do you want to stay for a little while or are you ready to go?"

"I'm ready if you are," Cardan replies.

"See you at breakfast," Elena says before walking away.

"I'm leaving too," Dee announces, but she doesn't move an inch, just looks at me longingly. "I can't believe some people I know organized a breakfast at nine tomorrow…" Then rolls her eyes at Erin and Gabriel who look at her smiling broadly.

"That's because we're leaving at noon," my brother replies with a shrug.

"Anyway… I'm wasted," she adds, but doesn't move.

"For God's sake," Gabriel scolds me exasperated. "Take your woman to bed before she collapses right here."

Well, I was trying to behave, but if he insists…

"What do you want to do tomorrow after breakfast?" We have plenty of time before dinner.

"Stay in bed with you," she finally replies.

"Really?"

"Don't play coy, Martin, you want the same."

I just smile, maybe other stuff is in order too.

We just finished breakfast with the family. "I have a surprise for you.

"Don't bother guessing. You have no idea, *cariño,*" I say at her questioning look and take her hand to guide her to the hotel's reception. "I just need to go to the front desk for a moment, wait for me here."

Dee stays by the windows while I go to the concierge's desk to ask for the sleigh I rented for the day. This will be fun, and as much as I love being naked and in bed with her, I also want to venture out and do other stuff. Plus, we don't have snow in Silicon Valley.

With our arms around each other, we walk to the sports club at the other side of the resort. At the bottom of the entryway, I stop to kiss her. Her lips open and her tongue starts dancing with mine when a voice startles us.

"I knew it," I hear David saying. "I fucking knew it."

He's glaring daggers in our direction. And he isn't alone, behind him is my father, Cardan, and Elena.

"What do you want, David?" I'm ready for this. No more hiding.

"What are you doing with my woman?" he counters.

"She's not yours anymore," I reply, ready to get straight to the point, but Dee's hand over my chest stops me.

"I got this," she says softly. "David, I'm not yours. The sooner you accept that, the better."

But my brother ignores her and shouts, "I wasn't rich enough, eh? And you went searching for a bigger fish, I see."

"David," my father warns him.

"What? I'm sure you've heard her conversations with Elena? Destinee was always talking about landing a sugar daddy. Seems like her wish was granted."

David is out of his fucking mind. This needs to end—NOW!

"David, stop!" Destinee pleads.

"What?" he replies. "Are you playing the pregnancy card to trap him too?"

My mind goes blank for a second.

"What?" Lena, my father, and I blurt out at the same time. What is he saying?

Destinee looks as if a brick wall has fallen over her, my grasp over her hand tightens.

"She hasn't told you?" David snarls with a smirk. "Of course she didn't. She got pregnant and tried to tie me down with that. I told her I didn't believe it was mine, so I didn't want it."

This fucker…

I open my mouth to say something, but Lena is in front of Dee asking her already. "Is that true? What happened?"

"I offered her the money for a termination," David adds as if it were something to be proud of. "The bitch didn't accept it, and weeks after, she said she lost it."

"What?" My voice sounds loud and clear. Then I remember Dee saying something about a secret between them both. Something big and unforgivable. The pieces are falling into place.

"No one wants a whore as the mother of his kids, or wife in any case."

Why doesn't David shut the hell up?

"But seems like you're more stupid than I thought, Bro."

"*David, es suficiente,*" my father shouts in Spanish. That's enough.

"Why are you so upset?" I ask him. I don't understand his demeanor.

"Because she's a good fuck," David shrugs. "And no one leaves my bed until I say so."

Destinee is crying while Elena hugs her tight. And when I try to embrace her, she recoils.

*"Cariño…"*

"The cat is out of the bag," she whispers. "I was never trying to keep it from you, Martin," Destinee adds and the sadness in her voice almost breaks me.

"I know and I don't care about that," I tell her the truth. I'm sure there are a lot of gaps in that story, and I want to hear it coming from her lips.

"I can't stand between two brothers," she whispers when I reach for her face to dry her teary eyes. "I can't. This is bigger than us."

"Nothing is bigger than my love for you," I try to kiss her, but she leans back. "'I'll' always choose you, I want a life with you. I only care about you and…"

Then something hits me and my world becomes black.

# CHAPTER TWENTY-FOUR

*Destinee*

It isn't fair that you ran away when I couldn't stop you.

Where are you? We need to talk.

I love you, Destinee.

Come back to me.

Come back to us.

I've read and re-read Martin's email for the last three hours. My heart aches with every word, but even after reading it, I couldn't find the strength to hit reply.

From the moment I left the Lake Tahoe resort drowning in a sea of shame—I ran to my room, packed and rented a car. I've been hiding here in Petaluma in my aunt Daisy's home. My phone has been turned off since then. I bet if I turn it on, the damn thing would explode with messages from Martin, Lena, and even David. If only I was willing to talk to them.

I was the girl who looked like she was trying to trap not one, but two of them. I've known the Posadas for a long time, they are all as thick as thieves. In a situation like this one, my bets are they are keeping a united front. I'm not one of them, as much as my heart wishes for it. And for a family as close as they are, blood is thicker than water.

What could I say? Hey, I was pregnant with your brother's baby. He didn't want it, I did. He thought I got pregnant by another man to trap him. He offered the money for a termination, but I was incapable of doing it. I wanted the baby, even if I was destined to be a single mother. It didn't matter. I was in love with my little pea.

But as all good things happen in my life, it didn't last. Two weeks after the happy news, I woke up with cramps and bloodstained sheets. After running to the ER, my doctor announced my endometrium was too thin and it wouldn't be able to support a growing baby. That day I cried my eyes out, I called David from the hospital and begged him to come be with me. I needed him by my side offering me some comfort. He didn't even pick up the phone nor did he reply to my desperate texts. The moment the doctor discharged me from the hospital, my mind was made. A change was needed, it was impossible for me to heal in the same environment that hurt me. I started looking for a new job in a new city and well… you know the rest.

Now, I'm here, like an ostrich with my head in the sand. Risking my job again. On Monday, I called my boss to give him my notice, graciously, he gave me the entire week to think about my resignation. Today is Thursday, my time is running out, and I haven't decided yet.

I've cried a thousand rivers, I don't think there is a tear left to shed. But the deep sadness is still there. Filling every pore. I should have told Martin the night I went to his apartment looking for him. Before things between us got too deep. Yes, I blame myself for being a coward. A big fat chicken. In my defense, let's say I was too crazy for him, craving the feel of his arms around me again. Love and lust are powerful distractions.

The front doorbell rings bringing me back to the present. And reality. My aunt is at work, so I'm home alone and can't remember if she said something about someone coming. Maybe some girl scouts are here, my mouth waters at the thought. Just what my body is craving, some cookies.

Grabbing my wallet, I walk to the door looking forward to seeing a little child in a green and khaki uniform. But the man standing in front of me is anything but little.

"Martin," I say while my gaze takes him in. There's a cast on his wrist, a bruise on his chin, and a grim expression greets me. And my guilt grows by miles.

What happened between him and his brother? Was all of this because of me?

Did he come to stamp a big A on my forehead?

"What are you doing here?" *And how did you find me*, I want to add.

"I was looking for you," he replies, his lips in a hard line. "Why else would I be here?"

"You shouldn't have…" I start to say and at the same time, he comes forward two steps. His work boots in front of my Chucks. "Look, I'm sorry for everything. I know…"

Then he places a finger over my lips, silencing me.

"I don't care about anything but you," he says.

"Martin, after everything David said I…"

"You what, Destinee?"

"How could I look you in the eye? How could I stand in front of your father? In front of Lena?"

Martin takes my face between his hands. "That's enough, no more running. Right now, you will listen to me. Then you're packing your shit and coming back home with me."

"Martin, I can't."

"Why not?"

"I can't stand between you and your brother," I tell him. "Look at you. If I stay away, I'm sure with time you and David will talk and eventually everything will be alright…"

"I don't want to talk to him," he states. "I just need to talk to you."

Without waiting for an invitation, he walks inside the house as if he owns the place.

Ok, this will be hard, but I think I can do this. I can have a conversation and end things like an adult.

"What happened to you?" I ask, pointing to the cast and then at the bruise on his gorgeous face.

"It doesn't matter," he replies.

"It matters to me."

"David tackled me," he huffs out. "I hit my head against the stone steps and ended up with a concussion. I woke up in the hospital, and since then I've been looking for you everywhere."

Guilt gnaws at me

"Are you fine?"

"I am now," he replies. "I'm sorry, *cariño.*"

"Why are you saying that? It wasn't your fault. I was irresponsible and then…"

"Destinee, stop," he commands. "Stop and listen to me."

My mind is reeling, I can't think straight. Well, to be honest, I haven't been able to think straight for months now.

"Ok, tell me whatever you came here to say and leave."

"I'm not leaving without you."

My weak walls are crumbling. I'm like the little pig with a house made of straw. And he's the big bad wolf blowing it down. And yes, he's ready to devour me after. The look on his face says it all.

"Dee, if you're worried about my family. Don't be. Yes, they are concerned about a lot of stuff. David isn't acting right. They are also worried about you and everything you had to endure alone. My father said it was the first time he was ashamed of one of his kids. It was hard to hear."

"I'm sorry," I whisper. This relationship was a mistake from the very beginning.

"My father wasn't talking about me, Dee."

"Oh." It's the only thing I manage to say. Was his father talking about David?

"Then you disappeared. I looked for you everywhere. I went to your parent's, but no one said where you were."

"I left because I was the problem, I didn't know what else to do."

"You weren't the problem, Destinee."

I can't think straight. It was easier when I was by myself, throwing a pity party for one. I turn to look around my aunt's living room, when my gaze stops on Martin's intent expression.

"You know what your problem is, you're always running," he accuses me. "Stop for a second and think. You can't stay here forever, Dee, you're isolating yourself. I understand if you need time to process what happened at the resort, but before you drown in your guilt and remorse, you need to know all the facts."

"What facts?"

He looks around, the couch is just a couple of steps away. "Can we sit?"

And the award for the worst host goes to... this isn't my home, but still. "Yes, of course."

We sit on the couch, I'm in one corner, with a pillow on my lap, shielding myself from his presence.

"So tell me the facts," I whisper.

"First, I'm not letting you ruin this between us just because you're afraid."

No, no. I'm a tough girl, I'm not afraid of anything. But I'm ashamed, that's different.

"Or ashamed..." Damn this man for knowing what I'm thinking.

"Martin, David was right. I wanted to trap him."

For a second, he looks like I've slapped him.

"No, I wasn't after his money. I joke around a lot with your sister, those conversations were just playful stuff between the both of us." Yes, any girl would pray for her Anastasia Steele miracle, to be Cinderella in her very own story. However, I never asked for a dime, I just wanted him to love me, to choose me. "I thought if we had a baby, he would stay with us forever. I thought a baby would solve all our problems."

"I know…" he says.

"But David deserted me, and that was the straw that broke the camel's back. After that, I couldn't stand to be close to him."

"That's understandable," Martin nods as tears fill my eyes.

"I feel so bad about your family and the situation I put you all in."

"Destinee, if you're talking about the pregnancy, it takes two to tango. You acted like an adult and my brother was a prick. I'm proud of you for ending your relationship, I wish I knew that before."

My stomach is in knots. "I know… I should have told…"

"Yes," he concedes, his brown eyes on me. His gaze is so strong and intense. "But that changes nothing. I. Want. You. Destinee. I want to make a life with you. I want to beat the shit out of my brother. David needs to smarten up before he ends up in a really shitty place."

Does Martin really still want me, after all this?

"Dee, come back with me," he pleads. "Come back home, *cariño*. If you want space, you can stay at the apartment. I'll stay at a hotel or something."

"But Martin, that's your home…"

"I love you, what is mine is yours too." He undoes me like no other and then puts the pieces back together again.

"Dee, I was—*I am*—serious. The day at the resort, I had a ring in my pocket."

Oh my God... *what?*

"I knew you weren't ready for a proposal," he says when notices my shocked face. "But the plan was to promise myself to you after talking with my family. Then do the same with your folks."

My excuses are running low. I'm not sure what else to say.

"Come back with me, Dee," he insists. "Come here, into my arms that want to hold you every night. Put your hands on the chest of the man whose heart beats just for you. Let me show you that dreams really can come true. Let me show you what love means." He pauses. "And turn your phone on. Elena is going crazy, needing to talk to you. She has been a mess, she feels like she's failed you."

"It wasn't Lena's fault. *I* chose not to tell her."

"I know," he says. "Elena loves you like a sister. Now she's just waiting for me to convince you and make it official."

For the first time in the past few days a smile takes over my face.

"How did you find me?"

He runs a hand over his face. "Desperate times calls for desperate measures. The email had an IP tracker."

My geek figured out a way to locate me.

"Ok," I finally say.

"Ok, what?"

"I'll go back with you." I got this, plus, my job is waiting for me.

Triumph overtakes his gorgeous features. Those brown eyes, bright and clear. God, I love him so much. I've missed him like crazy.

"But I'll stay at the pool house, there is no need for you to leave your home."

"It's too big and lonely without you anyway."

I stand, ready to pack my stuff and go back to the place where I belong. And I'm not talking about my rented house. Maybe I need to take this step by step. But I'm going back to him. I'm going back to my love.

While I'm in the room grabbing my stuff, Martin stays on the couch making some calls. I suspect he's talking with Elena.

My aunt comes in, almost fainting. "He's here, Dee."

"Yes, he's here."

"That's what a man in love does, girly. It doesn't matter how far you are, he turns the entire world upside down."

"I know." Those two words are heavy around me like a blanket. He came to get me, it took some time, but he found me anyway.

He tracked me down because he loves me.

He located me because he cares.

"I'll miss you." My aunt makes me pause as she hugs me hard. "This is always your home, you can come whenever you want to visit. And bring that gorgeous man of yours next time, ok?"

"I will."

"And I'll call your mother," she adds. "I'll tell her you'll be very busy tonight." My aunt wags her eyebrows suggestively, which causes me to want to throw a pillow at her head. I'm so *not* discussing my sex life with her.

Martin and I walk out of my aunt's home. He's carrying my bag with his good hand and the other is at the small of my back, guiding me softly to a black SUV I've never seen before.

"I can't drive," he explains while he opens the back door for me.

As soon as I'm seated in the vehicle, I turn my phone on and the damn thing blows up with messages and missed calls.

Most of them are from Martin, I can't count how many times he tried to contact me. My heart breaks for him. Desperation pours from every word he said.

There are also a lot of texts from Lena and a couple of voice messages. So, after breathing deeply, I hit her number and wait for her to pick up.

"I'd kill you, if I wasn't this happy to hear from you, Dee."

"I'm sorry, Lena. Everything happened so fast, and I wasn't thinking clearly."

"I understand the fear, Dee," she says. "I've learnt from my own experience that you can't let fear control your life. You only live once, my friend. Be happy, my brother loves you so much."

"I know," I whisper. "He came for me."

"I knew he would." Elena cries with so much happiness and I turn to look at Martin who's looking through the glass at the passing scenery.

"We're heading home now."

"Good," she says. "See you in a couple days, we're having lunch together on Sunday."

"Ok…" I reply hesitantly, but not in the mood to argue with her anymore.

"We have a lot to talk about, be ready!"

A couple of minutes after that we hang up. I bet my friend is ready to smack my head as soon as she's close, frankly, I feel like I deserve it.

I turn to look at Martin again, the man I love is stuck behind a wall I built because of my insecurities. I need to find a way to do what he did for me.

I need to find a way to fight for him.

When the driver parks in front of my home, Martin leans in to kiss me on the cheek before he hops out of the car to reach for my bag. "Don't you ever forget how much I love you," he says softly.

My heart sighs as I watch him drive off. I want to go back with him, but I just need to figure out my own path to follow.

For me.

For us.

# CHAPTER TWENTY-FIVE

*Martin*

I feel better today, even after another sleepless night, I'm myself again. I want to pound on Destinee's door and kiss her until her walls come down and her fears vanish. But even a geek like me knows that isn't the way this works.

I gotta be patient. I promised to give her the space she needs to heal and think about the whole situation. That means waiting. Again.

Fuck.

I'm a man of action, this 'stay here and see what happens' is killing me. So I bury my head in work. What else am I going to do?

My head isn't hurting anymore, but my sprained hand is slowing me down and that infuriates me. My assistant is hiding behind her desk, trying not to make any noise. For a woman who's used to blasting P!nk all day long, it's a miracle.

Aiko, the girl from San Diego, is finally coming on board with my app design. It should be ready in a couple of months. I'm sure it will be a success, the concept is smart and the interface is really easy to use. People around the globe will be paying thousands just to be on there and find their perfect match. Aiko will be a very wealthy woman in no time at all.

A knock on my door makes my head jerk up, just when I was starting to get engrossed in my production report for the past quarter.

"Come in," I call out and my eyes almost pop out of my head when I see who's standing there with a shy smile and a huge paper bag hanging from one of her hands.

"Are you busy?" she asks.

"Not at all," I reply as I push out my chair and walk to welcome her.

While I get closer to her and take in her beauty, I have to restrain myself from grabbing and kissing her properly. Or taking advantage of the short skirt she's wearing by laying her on my desk.

And fuck me, those over the knee boots...

"I'm sure you're wondering what I'm doing here, right?" she says after a short silence.

"Yes," I manage to reply.

"Your tech tour kinda sucked," she adds. "You never brought me to your office."

That makes me smile, her sass never gets old.

"You came just for a tour?" I ask, lifting my eyebrows.

"And to invite you for lunch," Dee replies as she shows me the paper bag in her hand. Well, that makes sense. Sort of. "Are you hungry?"

*Yes, but not for food.* I want to say, but my stomach growls, making her giggle a little.

Destinee gets busy setting the table for two, and I entertain myself ogling her. The hem of the mini thing she's wearing lifts every time she bends over the table. I'm pretty sure I caught a glimpse of lace under the fabric. While my heart is beating hard against my ribs, in my mind I can't stop questioning why she's really here.

"Greek salad and gyros," she announces, pointing to the table. "I hope you approve."

"Of course, thank you."

A very awkward silence descends upon us while we start eating. There is too much for us to talk about, however, I'm allowing her to set the pace.

"I like your office," she says in a little voice.

My office is modern and sleek. I hired an interior designer who did a great job here, and years after that, I hired him again to help me to decorate my apartment.

"It suits me," I reply with a shrug.

"This is hard for me," she finally says. "All this relationship stuff, I mean."

"Got it."

"Because it's not that simple for me to assume after everything that things will be easy. After so many years with David, the pregnancy, the way it ended. And the fact that he's your brother. How can your family not be stuck in the middle of this mess?"

I lean back in my chair. Thinking about what to say. For me she's making a mountain out of a molehill, but I wouldn't dare say I understand how the female brain works.

"My family supports us," I say because it's the truth. My father wants to apologize to Destinee *and* her family. Elena wanted to throttle David. By the time I woke up in the hospital I was ready to beat the shit out of him, too.

"I told my parents today I'm in love with you."

Thank fuck I'm sitting, my knees buckle in relief and my heart is running a mile a minute. But before my brain processes what it means for us, the need for clarification from her is overwhelming.

"What does that mean for us, Dee?" I look at her gorgeous silvery blue eyes. They are shining, warm and clear.

"It means I want to go ahead with you at full force," she breathes. "Maybe you should meet my therapist, but I'm ready for this to happen, Martin. Really…"

Sick of waiting any longer, I'm on her before she can finish speaking. I grab her, and turn her around to kiss her in a fiery crash of lust and love. A gasp leaves her sweet mouth at the first touch of my tongue over hers and then our hands are gripping each other looking for naked skin.

Since I'm sporting a cast on my left wrist, I'm not wearing a suit today, just a Henley and jeans. In a blink of an eye, Destinee's skirt is around her waist and her lacy panties hanging from one of her ankles. I slip my good hand up her thighs to her warm pussy, and I push my middle finger into her. She's so wet it slides in easily, as she grips me tight, moaning from the feeling. I pull my lips away from hers just enough to look into her eyes.

"We'll be happy together, Dee. Forever."

"Yes," she cries out loud hanging from my shoulders while pleasure takes over her body.

I'm not sure if she's accepting because of the ecstasy controlling her or if she believes it. We'll have time to talk about it later. We have all the time in the world. The future awaits us.

My hands are back on her thighs as I look down at her gorgeous face. "If you don't want this…"

In response she tugs on the button of my jeans and zipper, taking my hard cock out and placing it at her entry. "I want this," she whispers. "Give me what's mine."

Her eyes are wild and her face is flushed as I press my lips over hers, taking her sweet body in one hard thrust.

"So good, *cariño*. So fucking good."

She moans a little as I rotate my hips in the way I know she likes. Her grip on my shoulders tightens while she drops her head back.

"I love you," she murmurs, her words are my undoing. Emotion crashes through me. And I need to stay focused in the moment, to get her off first. I won't finish until she comes at least twice. "Fuck, how I love you."

Her body milks mine and I let go. Fate played with us, tearing our paths apart, but what is written in the starts sooner or later finds its way to be—we're destined.

This, between us is mad, passionate, and genuine. There aren't enough words to describe our love. It's beyond that. I have more love for her than there are stars in the sky.

# EPILOGUE

*Destinee - Seven years later*

"Are we watching the movie again, Mommy?" Liah, my almost four-year-old daughter asks me pointing at the little USB in my hands. It's a tradition, every year on our anniversary Martin and I start the celebration by watching our wedding day video.

When Liah was born, we decided to incorporate her into our festivities.

"Let's do it now," she whispers conspiratorially. "Before Luca wakes up."

Luca is our three-month-old son. He has a good set of lungs, if he wakes up hungry or with a wet diaper, he will let us know about his discomfort.

"Say, yes! Mommy, please!"

Ugh, she knows I can't refuse her when she looks at me with those big blue puppy-dog eyes. Liah has dark hair, and looks like the spitting image of her father. But she has inherited my eyes, and my husband says my sassiness too.

"We need to wait for *papá*, he will be here soon, baby. Just a couple more hours." In a toddler language that means an eon.

Martin had a meeting with some new investors in London yesterday, he called a couple of hours ago before boarding a private plane to come home.

"If he's almost home, we can just watch… but skip the kiss… it's so yucky."

"You think we're gross?" I ask her.

"So gross," she replies.

"You want to see your *papá* kissing other girls or not kissing in general?"

"Mommy, I never said I want *papá* kissing other girls. No. I'm just *asking* for you not to kiss so much."

This girl. She's definitely the brunette version of me.

"What if while waiting for *papá* we start with the albums? Pictures are as good as a video, right?"

"Ok, Mommy."

I take the big black book from one of our built-in shelves and we sit on a couch in a corner of our room, facing the backyard and trying to make as little noise as possible because Luca is a light sleeper.

"Look at your dress," my daughter says. Her little fingers are touching the picture softly, as if she were caressing the delicate fabric of my gown. "Mommy, would you wear it for me?"

I look at her beautiful face for a minute without knowing how to answer. I haven't worn my wedding dress since the day we were married. And after having kids, my body has changed a lot. My boobs aren't as perky as they were in those days and my tummy isn't that flat anymore. Yoga has helped. But Luca was born just three months ago and I can guarantee I don't fit in my old jeans yet. I've been wearing leggings around the house almost everyday since and for our little romantic date tonight I bought a dress with a lot of layers to help hide all the extra weight I've gained since my first pregnancy. I love my kids and I'm not ashamed of any of my stretch marks or the C-section scars. I wear those proudly, it's a daily reminder I've been blessed twice. But I'm still a woman, and this woman sometimes misses her pre-pregnancy body.

"Liah... I don't know where it is." I hope that's a good enough excuse.

"Oh, I know..." My girl jumps from the couch and marches to my walk-in closet. "Mommy, come on, I found it!"

I better hurry up and follow her, before her voice wakes up Luca.

"Here it is!" Liah yells again. "I found it, Mommy."

"Shh," I try to quiet her. "Your brother is sleeping, Liah!"

She closes her rosy mouth but is still jumping up and down while yanking the white zipper bag where my dress is stored safely.

"How did you know it was here?" I ask her while taking the bag off the rack and open it to take the dress out.

"Mommy, you have so many pretty dresses, I like to come in here and dream I'm tall like you and then I can wear them all."

Martin has to attend so many functions, with investors, partners… the list is endless. My wardrobe has to accommodate the occasions, and my man loves to make sure his wife always has the best of the best.

"One day you will be, baby," I tell her, touching her plump cheek.

Her eyes light up with happiness. "Yay!"

She starts jumping around the room again.

"Liah," I say after an idea comes to mind. "Why don't you wait for me on my bed while I change and do my hair?"

"Ok, Mommy," she squeals and runs to my room, thirty seconds later, a Disney song fills the space.

I strip my clothes off and hold the dress. The fabric is so beautiful and brings back so many great memories. Martin's face when he saw me walking down the aisle. The way he kissed me when the minister pronounced us man and wife. The things he whispered in my ear while we danced to our first song…

My wedding was a dream that became true in every sense. I look at my left hand and the ring that's there, shining in the daylight. Two dragonflies with a big central diamond are the symbol of his love for me. All the promises he made the day he kneeled in front of me and asked me to be his wife. Everyday since then I've felt like the luckiest girl in the entire world. Martin and I had our share of ups and downs, but we navigated through them together. Trusting in us and the bond between us.

Five minutes later I'm in front of the mirror, the dress surprisingly fits. I mean, the zipper is up, even if my boobs are about to burst the seams and it's tight around my waist. Taking the flatiron, I start to do my hair. Liah is busy watching Cocomelon, which gives me a little time to create some waves in my hair, and place the little crystals combs on one side of my head. I even had time to apply some makeup.

I look for the same royal blue heels I wore that day and walk into the room.

"How do I look?" I ask my daughter, but I stop in my tracks.

She isn't alone anymore.

*"Cariño,"* A hoarse voice mumbles in front of me, just a couple of feet away.

Martin is there, looking as gorgeous as ever—glasses and all. In one of his hands he's clutching a huge bouquet of red roses and with the other, he's holding our daughter.

"You're here," I manage to say while running toward him.

"Just one kiss," our daughter squirms between us, scolding us.

"But, baby," Martin says. "Today is our anniversary."

Liah rolls her blue eyes and gets down from her father's arm.

"Look, *papá!*" She cries out while jumping around me. "Mommy looks like a princess."

"You're my princess," he replies to her, but his hot gaze is on me. Making my skin burn, some things never change, and I hope they never will. "Mommy is my queen."

Martin places the flowers in my hands and at the same time our lips touch, and the promise of just a little kiss is forgotten.

"Happy anniversary, my love," he whispers. "I came home early to surprise you, but it seems like you were two steps ahead of me, as always."

We kiss until a loud cry resonates through the monitor. "Seems like someone wants to join the party," I say with a laugh.

"*Papá* is here, now it's movie time," Liah cries.

"But first let me get your brother," I tell her.

"I'll get him," Martin says. "You relax, and don't you dare take off that dress."

Five minutes later the four of us are in front of the TV, Martin feeds Luca while Liah is dancing in front of us, cheering when something happens in the video, all the while I'm leaning against my husband.

I love moments like this, not just celebrating our old memories, but creating new ones. Soon the scene of our first dance comes on the screen. Martin and I were in our own bubble, eyes just for each other, cherishing the bliss.

For a moment the camera focused on David—yes, as in Martin's brother—after a few complicated months, he decided to come and celebrate with us. It was so important for my husband and his family, and the olive branch he offered to us that day opened a new chapter in their relationship. David is staring at us, looking so damn heartbroken. It crushes me in some way, not because I still love him but because I've never wished any ill-will toward him. Gabriel came behind David and said something just for his ears and soon the cameraman focused on us again.

Luca finishes his bottle and while Martin leans him against his shoulder, he hugs me tighter to his other side. This is my life now, so full of love. Finding happiness in moments like this, just sitting with my family around me. Every time I put my head on his chest, I'm asking him without any words to keep my heart safe. And he does. But more than that, I had to learn how to fight and grow. I had to change, learn how to love myself and then to give him my entire heart.

Just like a dragonfly symbolizes change, the kind of change that understands the deeper meaning of life… I've found that change here, just being me—with my children—in the arms of the love of my life.

# THE END

The *secret* to change
is to focus all your **energy**
no ot on *fighting* the old

but on *building*
**the new**

# Happy GIRLS ARE THE Prettiest ♡

—Audrey Hepburn

# ACKNOWLEDGEMENTS

What a year, right?

I want to start by thanking God for blessing me and for giving me strength and inspiration between so many changes in my life lately.

To my girl, thank you, niña, for all the help!

To my family, without them I would not be doing this, they have always been the reason behind all my work.

To the amazing Ariadna Basulto, the most chingona PA ever.

To my girls Dar and Athena, thank you for your support and for giving this story the polish to make it shine. I couldn't do it without you, YOU'RE AMAZING. To Celia, this one is for you and your big heart. Crystal thank you so much for being such an amazing beta. And to my music fairy ♥. Thank you, girls!

To my group the **Lollipop Gang**, girls, you're the BEST. Love you! To my **Goal Diggers**, my ST. You're a blessing to me, **THANK YOU!!**

To my friends, because they are the best cheerleaders in the world, thanks for the extra strength, the prayers, the laughter, the patience, and the unconditional support.

To my soulmate authors, love you! You have been so amazing to me.

Thank you, Josette and Charlotte, from Grey's PR. To all the bloggers and Insta-bloggers, for their support and for giving the opportunity to showcase my work. THANK YOU!

Thanks, y'all, for supporting me with your sweet messages, I can't put into words how much that means to me.

Thank you for reading and support this job I love so much, means the world to me.

From the bottom of my heart… Thank you!

*S x*

# ABOUT THE AUTHOR

Susana Mohel is a *USA Today* best-selling author whose stories sizzle like the sunshine in her Southern California mountains.

Her fast-paced, angsty contemporary romance novels transport readers to a world of spunky heroines and hunky heroes who find their way to a happily ever after... with plenty of spiced-up moments along the way.

When she's not writing, Susana can be found wandering the trails along with her husband or creating chaos in her garden.

www.susanamohel.com

# BOOKS BY SUSANA MOHEL

Read free with Kindle Unlimited!

**Whispers of My Skin**

(A second-chance, western standalone romance)

**Rainstorm – Chase & Rose**

(A second-chance, standalone romance)

**Blank Spaces – Lancelot & Ariel**

(A enemies-to-lovers, standalone romance)

**Off Limits – Adrik & Jordania**

(A forbidden/military, standalone romance)

**Blurred Lines – Evan & Morgana**

(A Reverse Age-Gap, standalone romance)

**Beyond our Forever – Bruce & Ilythia**

(A second-chance, standalone romance)

**Fated**

**Cardan & Elena**

(A small-town/Age-gap standalone romance)

**Wrecked**

**Ella & David**

(A small-town/second-chance romance)

**Wanted:** A Salvation Society Novel

Lionel &Stella

(A Romantic Suspense, standalone romance)

**Unexpected Savior:** A Cocky Hero Club Novel

Nicolaus & Gina

(A second-chance, standalone romance)

**Uncovering Hope**

(An Office standalone romance)